In the bedroom, she pulled from the trunk a lacy nightgown made especially for this night together.

It was long and flowing, with ribbons closing the neck.

She prepared carefully, brushing her hair until it gleamed with indigo shadows. She studied her reflection in the mirror. Did Caleb see how much she loved him? She straightened. She had every intention of making her love quite plain to him.

She returned to the other room. "Caleb?"

He sat in the rocker, staring at the lamp. At her voice, his head jerked up.

"I'm ready for bed."

The taut muscles in his jaw drew deep hollows in his cheeks. "You go ahead," he muttered. "I'll be along later."

She sighed. . . . "For two years I have lived for the time we could curl into each other's arms. . . . I have clung to the memory of the three days we spent together. . . ."

"We aren't the same two people. Those people were young and innocent."

"Yes, we've had to grow up in a way our parents didn't have to. But inside I'm still the same. I believe you are, too. Still full of dreams. Gentle. Kind."

"No. That man died back in France."

She nodded. He was partially right. He had changed. "The changes are simply layers that add maturity and depth."

"I wish I could believe you're right." He stared into the darkness and shuddered.

"I know I'm right." She laughed. "You'll have to trust me on this one."

LINDA FORD draws on her own experiences living in the Canadian prairie and Rockies to paint wonderful adventures in romance and faith. She lives in Alberta, Canada, with her family, writing as much as her full-time job of taking care of a paraplegic and four kids who are still at home will allow. Linda says, "I thank God that He has given me a full, productive life and that I'm not bored. I thank Him for placing a little bit of the creative energy revealed in His creation into me, and I pray I might use my writing for His honor and glory."

Books by Linda Ford

HEARTSONG PRESENTS
HP240—The Sun Still Shines
HP268—Unchained Hearts
HP368—The Heart Seeks a Home
HP448—Chastity's Angel
HP463—Crane's Bride

Lizzie

Linda Ford

Heartsong Presents

Dedicated to my parents, who taught me to love God's gifts and trust Him for life's necessities.

A note from the author:
I love to hear from my readers! You may correspond with me by writing:

> Linda Ford
> Author Relations
> PO Box 719
> Uhrichsville, OH 44683

ISBN 1-58660-766-9

LIZZIE

one

Alberta, Canada—March 1919

Twenty-three-year-old Elizabeth Hughes leaned close to the train window, her breath fogging the smoky pane. "What if he's not here?"

Her travelling companion, Maryelle, squeezed her hands. "Don't look so scared."

"It's been two years."

The last time she'd seen Caleb, they'd been married exactly three days and four hours and had spent the time in a little cottage in the English countryside, getting to know each other as man and wife and enjoying themselves immensely. It about tore her heart out to say good-bye to him as he boarded the train bound for France.

There had been letters, of course. She smiled. A great deal more letters from her than from him. And his always so short. As the days passed, even the word or two of love stopped, and his messages grew terse. "Rain here. Mud everywhere. When will this end?"

She cried when his letters came. It was like walking on hot coals to think of him suffering the mud and disease of the trenches. And all that death.

She could do nothing but weep and pray.

Maryelle stretched and yawned. "It's almost time."

Lizzie nodded, her throat too tight to speak. She'd waited so long. The war had finally ended. Strange, though, how everyone seemed so weary they sort of sat down with a huge sigh. It took time before they slowly picked themselves up and started putting the pieces of life back together. Only to get knocked flat again by the influenza epidemic.

Father had refused to let her travel during the epidemic, even though she had begged when news came that Caleb had been deployed home in January. February was almost over before he decreed it was safe enough to travel. He'd arranged for Maryelle, another war bride, to travel with her. Lizzie didn't envy Maryelle the hours she had left to travel. Already this trip had gone on forever.

Maryelle grabbed Lizzie's bags and handed them to her. "Now you go and find that man of yours."

Lizzie paused. "You'll write?"

"As soon as I can."

Lizzie stepped from the train. She looked up and down. There was no one in the shivering darkness. "He's not here," she whispered. Then she saw a shadowy figure climb the steps at the far end. Boots thudded across the planks in her direction.

Too dark to make out his features, she knew it was Caleb by the way he walked. Her insides turned to pudding; her legs threatened to melt under her. Then, with a choked cry, she threw herself into his arms, clinging to him, weeping shamelessly.

He held her close.

She took a shuddering breath and sniffed a time or two before she lifted her face. "Caleb, I thought I would never get here."

"You're here now. That's all that matters."

She tilted her chin and stretched until their lips met. The station door opened, throwing a cone of light across the wooden platform; a trolley rattled toward the luggage car, but Lizzie didn't care. She had waited too long to put this off anymore.

He leaned into the kiss, warming her lips, flooding her heart with heat.

When they finally pulled apart, she murmured, "I thought I'd never see you again." She planted kisses all over his face. "You taste so good. I will never be able to get enough of you." She leaned back against his embrace and drank in the sight of him. "You're thin." His eyes were sunken, his face drawn. He was only twenty-four, but he had the features of a man decades older. "You've suffered," she whispered, an arrow piercing her heart.

"I've been at war," he muttered.

"Thank God it's over. Now we can get on with the business of living." She kissed him again.

"It's late and cold. We'd best be getting home."

"Home. I like the sound of that. You and me together at last." She stepped back. "You're right. Let's go home."

It took a moment to load her trunks in the wagon; then Caleb helped her to the seat and tucked a warm fur blanket around her.

"How far is it?" she asked.

"Not far."

"I've heard that so often the past few days. Sometimes it means a mile, sometimes a hundred." She laughed. "Please tell me it's not a hundred."

"It's not a hundred." She could hear the smile in his voice. "But it's not one either. It's two."

She laughed merrily. "Two I can live with, thank you, Mr. Hughes." She cradled the name to her heart. Mr. Caleb Hughes, husband, and Elizabeth Anne Hughes, wife. What a delicious thing this union was. She pressed herself to his side, revelling in the feel of him after so many months of nothing but dreams.

It might have been a short trip, but Lizzie's sleepless nights of anticipation had taken their toll. By the time Caleb reined in before a dark building, fatigue had robbed her of the ability to think. He practically carried her to the door, steadying her as he lit a lamp. She didn't even look around. As long as there was a bed, it was all she cared about. She swayed and moaned. A chair bumped the back of her knees, and gentle hands pushed her to the seat.

"I'll be right back," Caleb said.

Lizzie couldn't keep her eyes open. *How strange,* she mused. All evening she had tried to sleep, and her eyes refused to close. Now, when she was determined to remain awake until she could get her fill of looking at Caleb, her eyes wouldn't stay open. Maybe her eyes understood she would never get enough of looking at him.

The sweep of cold air announced his return. "I'm very tired," she said, her words slurred.

"It would appear so." He unbuttoned her coat and pulled her arms out, removed her shoes and peeled off her stockings. He slipped her dress over her head and settled a nightdress on her, then carried her to the bed. She curled against him, pressing her face into the hollow of his shoulder. A sigh came from somewhere deep inside.

"I am so glad I'm finally here," she murmured, her voice thick with fatigue. She didn't know if he answered before she fell asleep.

⁂

The gray morning light sifted through a dusty window, crossed Lizzie's eyes, and wakened her. Consciousness came in a bolt, and she turned to greet Caleb.

His side of the bed was empty.

She threw back the covers and jumped from bed. "Ah, cold," she muttered as her feet touched the bare wood.

Hopping across the floor, she stepped into the other room where Caleb stood over the stove. Reluctant warmth edged toward the bedroom. "Good morning, Mr. Hughes," she called, hurrying to his side, spreading her hands to greet the warmth above the stove. "How did you sleep?"

"Good morning." He shoved another chunk of wood into the stove, dusting his hands on his pants before he turned to study her. "You seem well rested."

She stretched her hands over her head and arched her back, yawning widely. "Feel fit as a fiddle." She draped her hands around his neck. "Kiss me."

He bent his head, and their lips met. The kiss lasted only a moment. She clung to him, wanting a taste of the passion they'd shared on their honeymoon. When he made no effort to kiss her again, she wrapped her arms around herself and faced the stove. "Cold morning, isn't it?"

"Spring is reluctant this year." He stood with his hands shoved into the back pockets of his trousers. "Good thing you waited until now to travel. February was miserable."

He sounded almost pleased about the month of bad weather. His finely chiselled features were sharpened by his thinness. The hollows under his eyes caught the shadows of the room in pools of inky darkness. His hair—dark and wavy—remained his best feature. "I would have come anyway except for the flu," she said.

"Good thing you didn't."

"Didn't you miss me?"

"Of course I missed you. But it was a good thing you never faced the temperatures of February. The thermometer dropped to minus forty for most of the month."

A shiver raced up her spine at the darkness in his eyes. "I wouldn't have liked that."

"I have chores to do." He crossed the room and pulled on a heavy coat and overboots. "I'll be back in about an hour."

Chill air raced across the room, and she dashed for the bedroom door.

One of her trunks sat at the end of the bed; and she threw it open, pulled out warm stockings, a woolen skirt and jumper, and put them on. She smoothed the pile of quilts on the bed, then hurried back, suddenly eager to see her new home more closely.

Beside the stove, now humming as it kicked out a blast of heat, stood a wooden table, four mismatched chairs, and a narrow cupboard. Across the room, a worn burgundy sofa sagged toward the floor next to a wooden rocker with peeling paint. Empty bookshelves lined the wall. The whole room would have fit into their kitchen back home in Britain, but she hugged herself and smiled widely.

"Home, sweet home," she murmured. Her sister Patricia had cross-stitched a hanging with those very words for Lizzie to put in the house she would share with Caleb. She'd hang it up as soon as possible to prove she'd finally come home.

❧

Stacks of belongings surrounded her, when the door opened and Caleb stood before her, a bucket of milk in his hand. He looked about, his eyes troubled. "I'm sorry I don't have more to offer you than this mean shack." He set the pail on the table. "It's a poor home."

"Oh, no!" She sprang to her feet. "It's fine for the two of us, and it will fix up nicely. I was going through my things, deciding how to brighten the place. Thanks to Patty and Victoria, I have lots of pictures. Patty made this hanging.

Victoria painted these pictures of home."

Caleb took the pictures and studied them one by one. "Very nice."

"Vicky would be glad to hear you like them. She's never forgotten how you teased her for some of her imaginative work."

"Maybe your sister should have done some of those to send with you." He handed the pictures back to Lizzie.

Lizzie cocked her head. "I'm not sure what you mean."

"Nothing much. Just that it all seems sort of unreal."

"What exactly are you referring to?" She struggled to keep her voice low and calm as a thousand butterflies took flight in her stomach.

He lifted a crock from beside the cupboard and poured the milk into it. "My time in England, I suppose. Before I went to the Front."

"Would that include our marriage?"

"You could hardly call it a normal marriage." He fiddled with the now-empty pail.

Her stomach calmed, not a flutter of anything as she stared at his rigid back. "I don't know what you mean."

He looked at her, his expression dark, bottomless. "We were married all of three days. That was two years ago. Does that seem normal to you?" He turned away so she couldn't see him, couldn't face his questions, couldn't face his denial.

"It was normal enough for many couples during the war. I thought"—she gulped back tears—"I suppose I thought because I still love you and wanted nothing more than to be with you again that you would feel the same." Her voice fell to an agonized whisper.

He sighed. "All I mean is neither of us may be what the other remembers."

"Caleb, if you no longer love me, tell me. I can't stand not knowing."

He straightened and faced her squarely. "You are my wife. Of course I love you."

"Then hold me and kiss me and sound a little more convincing." She waited, forbidding herself to make the first move.

His jaw tightened, emphasizing the hollows in his cheeks. A shudder snaked across his shoulders. With a muffled groan, he pulled her to his chest and buried his face in her hair. "Don't pay me any attention, Lizzie. I don't know why I say the things I do."

She clung to him until he squirmed. "I suppose you'd like breakfast," she said, stepping away. "I see there're plenty of eggs." A wire basket on the cupboard held a half dozen. "No doubt that's one of the pleasures of living on a farm—lots of eggs and milk." She broke two eggs into a bowl.

"There'll be more eggs today."

She hesitated a moment, then broke two more and whisked them with a bit of milk. "Back home we were down to one egg a week. And nothing but tinned or powdered milk for so long I can't remember the taste of fresh milk."

"Lots of both here. Mother sees to that."

She stopped stirring the eggs. "When will I meet your parents? What do they think of me?"

He jerked his head toward the window. "They're just across the way."

She hurried to the window, rubbing away the film of dust. A big house stood on a rise, across a rutted trail and a wide expanse of brown grass. To her left stood a hip-roofed barn. A tan-colored cow chomped at her feed.

"We'll go over after breakfast."

She hurried to the stove to cook the eggs. In a few minutes, she set a plateful of food before each of them. Caleb offered a short grace. She added her own silent words, *Lord, help us find our way back to each other.*

His meal finished, Caleb tipped his chair back. "As soon as you're ready, I'll take you across to meet the folks."

"I'll do the dishes later."

"No need to hurry." He ambled over and pulled on his coat and boots.

Lizzie followed on his heels, slipping her arms through the sleeves of her coat. "I'm set."

Caleb took her hand as they stepped outside. The gesture comforted and strengthened her. She smiled into the morning sunshine. He would soon discover she hadn't changed, and he'd remember why he loved her.

"It's a fine morning," she said, filling her lungs with unfamiliar smells of fresh manure, hay, and the steaming earth.

"The sun is going to shine today." He lifted his face, closing his eyes. "The sun makes me feel good."

"It's lovely and warm. Makes me feel good just to be alive." She didn't mean the sunshine alone; her thoughts included the joy of being able to touch him and watch him.

He turned to her, his breath warming her cheeks as he murmured, "I'd forgotten your ready smile. I thought my memories were only a dream."

She tipped her head back, openly inviting him to see her love and faithfulness; but he shivered, and his eyes darkened. She felt a door close somewhere in his thoughts.

"Caleb," she murmured, wanting to call him back, but he stepped away.

"My folks are waiting."

"I'm eager to meet them." Whatever strange thoughts troubled Caleb, she knew he still loved her. She'd seen a spark in his eyes, the spark that had drawn her to him in the first place.

He led her to the large house and threw open the door, pulling her into a large farm kitchen with a long wooden table and rows of cupboards with bottles and crocks lining the top. A monstrous stove belched in the corner. The house was rich with scents—yeasty bread, warm milk, and a hint of some cleaning compound.

Caleb drew her toward the table. "Mother, Dad, this is my wife, Elizabeth."

A small woman, dressed all in black from the choker-tight collar at her neck to the closely buttoned sleeves at her wrists to her skirt, rose and gave Lizzie a brisk hug. "Welcome, Elizabeth."

Mother Hughes released her. Father Hughes closed his Bible and took her hand. "Welcome to Alberta. I hope you like the place."

"It's vast and awe inspiring," Lizzie said. "And completely beautiful."

"Would you care for tea?"

Mother Hughes hurried to the side cupboard to get two cups. Lizzie was surprised to see the black skirts of her mother-in-law's dress went to the toes of her shoes.

"How was your trip?" Father Hughes asked.

"For the most part uneventful. But it seemed dreadfully long. I was grateful for a travelling companion."

Mother Hughes placed a cup before her and another in front of Caleb. "I didn't know you were travelling with someone. Somehow I thought you'd be unescorted."

Lizzie smiled at her mother-in-law, her glance shifting to the framed Scripture verse on the wall behind the older woman. "Be sober, be vigilant; because your adversary the devil. . . walketh about seeking whom he may devour. 1 Peter 5:8."

She shifted her gaze back to Mother Hughes. "My parents wouldn't hear of it. Father arranged for another war bride to travel with me."

"Very wise." Caleb's father nodded approval.

Mother Hughes cleared her throat. "And how do you like your new home?"

"I haven't had time to get settled, of course." Lizzie reached for Caleb's hand. "But the house looks quite fine. After being separated for two years, I would live in a tent if it meant we could be together."

"I told Caleb there was plenty of room for you both in this house." Mother Hughes sighed heavily. "But he insisted on fixing up that old shack. It wasn't meant to be anything but temporary quarters for harvest help. But Caleb always seems to be glad of a chance to be on his own. Just like when he signed up for the war when he didn't have to."

Caleb's hand tightened on Lizzie's. She felt her eyes grow wide.

"Now, Mother," Father Hughes said, his voice gentle but slightly chiding. "I'm sure Caleb didn't sign up just to gain independence."

"Not many men went to war because they wanted to." Lizzie couldn't remain quiet when Caleb had been criticized. "They went to defend our freedom. Thank God that Caleb returned. And thank you for making me welcome and for inviting me to share your house, but I'm sure you'll understand how much I've ached to take care of Caleb. I'm anticipating being able to make his meals"—she laughed low in her throat—"though I don't claim to have any culinary skills. With rationing so tight, Mother said she couldn't afford to let us practice." Caleb's hand relaxed, giving her confidence to continue. "But my sisters and I managed to learn the basics."

A lump swelled in her throat as she thought of her sisters and parents. Suddenly she missed them more than she could imagine, and she bowed her head, holding back tears.

Caleb squeezed her hand. "It will be hard for Lizzie to be so far from her family."

"Lizzie? What a frivolous derivative of a beautiful biblical name."

"Frivolous?" Lizzie chuckled. "Not me. I'm the sober one of the bunch. I leave the frivolity to my sisters, Patricia and Victoria."

Caleb's deep chuckle rang in her ear. "Lizzie's sisters are probably responsible for my falling in love with her. When I saw how good-spirited she was with their shenanigans, I couldn't help but feel she was a special girl."

"You'll find things different here." Mother Hughes nodded briskly without a hint of a smile.

Her words carried an ominous warning, but Lizzie decided to remain lighthearted. "I'm sure I shall. But with your help I'm certain I'll learn and adjust."

"We'll help all we can, my dear," Father Hughes said, giving his wife a warning look.

They left a few minutes later, carrying a pot of stew and a slab of meat.

"Mother tends to be sharp at times," Caleb said as they returned to their own little house.

"Not to worry. I didn't take offense. Mother taught us life is too short to look for offense when none is meant."

"I remember her saying that more than once."

"Can you help me hang pictures?"

"I could spare a little time."

She hurried to the trunk. "I want to hang this 'Home, Sweet Home' sampler beside the door."

"I'll get a hammer and nails." He went outside, returning before she had chosen a place for the series of paintings Vicky had done. He hung the sampler, then turned to her for more instruction.

"Frames took too much room, but I don't know how to hang these without them."

"I could make some simple ones if you like."

"That'd be wonderful. But first look at these." She handed him some photos, pressing close as he studied them.

The first was a picture of her, her sisters, and Caleb, clustered around an oak tree. "That was the first time we went on a picnic together. Do you remember?"

"How could I forget?" He smiled as he ran his thumb along the edge. "I had never met anyone like your bunch. It was like being with an impromptu theater company."

"You made a very nice prince." At first he'd seemed a bit overwhelmed by the trio of sisters; then he joined in their fun with a gusto that made them all love him. She tipped her head to study him. "I still can't believe Father brought you home. It's so unlike him. I wonder why he did."

Caleb's eyes grew dark, unreadable. "Probably because he saw a country hick lost and alone."

"I think he saw something more than that." She hugged his arm. "He saw a warm, gentle man facing the horrors of war."

Caleb stepped back, but not before she felt him shudder. "I've got things to do. I expect you can manage the rest on your own." He yanked on his coat and strode out.

Lizzie rushed to the window. She expected him to go toward the barn or to his parents' house, but he headed down the road. She watched until he was out of sight before she turned back to the room. But her interest in the mementos of home had vanished. She set the pile of pictures aside and turned her attention to the stack of dirty dishes.

❧

With the corner of her apron, Lizzie wiped beads of sweat from her brow. She wanted this meal to be special—the first real meal she'd cooked for Caleb in their new home. But the stove proved uncooperative. She threw in a handful of wood, only to have the fire blaze so hot she burned the meat. And just when she wanted the water to boil for potatoes, the flames barely flared. Yet when she added more wood, the pot boiled so hard the potatoes turned to mush.

Caleb came in, the dark look in his eyes still lingering. He brought with him several lengths of narrow wood, and while she tried to salvage the meal, he measured the frames he had promised.

"I tried so hard to make this a special meal, but I can't seem to get the hang of the stove," she muttered, as she set what was still edible before Caleb.

"Looks fine to me." He dished up charred meat, watery potatoes, and lumpy turnips.

Lizzie watched in amazement as he ate the food without flinching. She tasted her own and grimaced. A burnt flavor permeated the meat. Despite her hunger, she had to choke it down.

"What did you do today?" She toyed with the food on her plate.

"Nothing special."

"Everything is new and special to me. I saw you walking down the road. Where did you go?"

"Mostly just walking." He ate as if his life depended on it.

She laughed. "Caleb, you don't have to pretend it's good. I know it isn't. But thank you for trying to make me feel better." She pushed back her chair and moved to his side.

Leaning over, she kissed his cheek.

"It's not that bad. After the food we ate—" He pushed his plate aside, a slow grin spreading across his face as he shoved his chair back and pulled her to his lap. "'Course the company here is a lot better."

She nuzzled against him. "Are you saying you'd sooner be with me than a bunch of muddy soldiers?"

His arms tightened around her. "I'd sooner be here with you than anyplace I can imagine." He shuddered once. "I'm so glad you're here."

"Me, too." And a thousand times more glad to hear him confess it. She turned her face toward him. He accepted her invitation and kissed her slowly and thoroughly. "I love you, Caleb. I've missed you so much I thought I would die." She hugged him hard enough to make him groan.

"I've missed you like crazy, too," he murmured.

She coiled her fingers in his dark curls and sighed. She had come home at last.

He looked deep into her eyes. "I fear life will be full of hardship for you here."

"Don't worry about it. I'm prepared to adjust. Besides, I'm not as coddled as you think. Things got difficult for everyone before the war ended. Food shortages, fuel shortages, and the long lists of casualties."

He set her aside and jerked to his feet. "War is hell on earth." He strode to the door. "I'll go fix those frames I promised you."

Shocked at his words and stunned by his sudden change in mood, she stared after him.

two

The sun dropped below the horizon, and only a steely gray light remained outdoors. She lit the lamps and waited for Caleb to return.

Suddenly he threw the door back and stepped inside. He stared at the lamp, his eyes wide and unfocused.

"It's a cool evening," Lizzie said.

He didn't turn toward her or even blink.

"Perhaps you could close the door, Caleb."

He jerked at the sound of his name. "Sorry." He kicked the door shut. "Are these all right?" He handed her four wide, wooden frames.

"They're perfect." She secured the paintings in the frames with the thin boards he had cut. "There. Don't they look fine? Where do you think we should hang them?"

"I suppose you want them where you can see them often. Reminders of home and all that."

"Caleb, they're for you as much as me. Reminders of when we met and fell in love. See this one?" She picked the one showing the trees at the back of the yard. "Remember the play we put on down there?"

He nodded. "We were full of stories of heroism and pride."

She chose another picture. "Here we are in the parlor. Vicky never could do faces very well; but if you look carefully, you can see it's the three of us." She lingered over the scene, remembering all the good times they'd had. "Of course, you have only to look at the musical instruments to know who each one is. Vicky's at the harp, Patricia's at the piano, and I'm playing my flute." She handed the picture to Caleb and chuckled. "And just to make sure, Vicky's titled the picture 'Beanie, Pete, and Bear.'"

The darkness in his expression faded, and he grinned. "I never could understand those silly nicknames you gave each other."

"Pete grew out of Patricia's name. And I guess because Vicky was the youngest, Patricia and I would say she was no bigger than a bean."

"And you?"

"I'm sure I've told you this before."

"If you did, I don't remember." His eyes twinkled.

Lizzie clung to his gaze. Oh, that look in his eyes! That look had captured her heart in the first place. "I suppose you could say Mother started it. One of the neighborhood boys teased Vicky one day, and I sprang to her defense." She looked away and mumbled, "Rather vigorously, you might say."

He chortled. "You beat up the little brat."

"You have too heard the story before."

"Parts of it, maybe. But how did that lead to your nickname?" She studied him suspiciously. "You're stringing me."

He held up his hands. "Honest. I don't remember the details."

"Mother said I defended her like a mother bear." She raced through the words.

He hooted. "Bear! I do believe I'd better be careful not to cross you."

"I was only about ten years old."

"Now you're twenty-three. I guess you'd be more than twice as fierce."

She remembered her inclination to defend Caleb when his

mother accused him of going to war simply to get away. She laughed. "I guess I tend to spring to the defense of those I love."

He caught her close and tweaked her nose. "Not a bad fault, I wouldn't think."

She showed him the next painting—one of her family home surrounded by flowers, groomed hedges, and green lawns.

"Your home." He shook his head. "You'll miss it greatly."

"It's my parents' home," she corrected gently. "I'll miss them and my sisters, but I chose you. I could never be content apart from you."

He took the last picture. "The lake."

She nodded. "I asked Vicky to do this specially for us. It's where you first told me you loved me."

"And where a week later I told you I would be shipped out in two weeks and asked if you would marry me before I left. It was such a rushed wedding."

"I wouldn't have had it any other way. I loved you then as I love you now. Neither of us knew what the future held, but I knew I wanted whatever time we could have together."

"No regrets?"

"Only one."

His eyes darkened.

She smiled. "That we missed out on the first two years of our marriage."

"We can never gain back those years."

"To have the future together is enough for me." She turned to study the room. "Let's hang them over the bookcase. They'll look good there."

He drove in the nails, then, wrapping his arm about her waist, stood at her side to admire them.

She pulled away first. "It's getting late. I think I'll get ready for bed." She turned away, hiding her hot cheeks, lest he guess why she chose to go to bed early.

In the bedroom, she pulled from the trunk a lacy nightgown made especially for this night together. It was long and flowing, with ribbons closing the neck.

She prepared carefully, brushing her hair until it gleamed with indigo shadows. She studied her reflection in the mirror. Did Caleb see how much she loved him? She straightened. She had every intention of making her love quite plain to him.

She returned to the other room. "Caleb?"

He sat in the rocker, staring at the lamp. At her voice, his head jerked up.

"I'm ready for bed."

The taut muscles in his jaw drew deep hollows in his cheeks. "You go ahead," he muttered. "I'll be along later."

She sighed. Later wasn't good enough. She stepped into the room and crossed to his side, plunking down on the sagging sofa and resting her hand on his knee. "I need you."

His nerves twitched beneath her hand.

"For two years I have lived for the time we could curl into each other's arms."

She could feel him returning to her and leaned closer, aching for him. "I have clung to the memory of the three days we spent together." She reached around him to the pile of photos and sorted through them until she found the one she wanted. "Here we are." In the photo, he smiled down at her with a heart so full of love, one could see it even through the medium of photography.

He took the picture and looked at it. Suddenly he smiled. "We had a good time, didn't we?"

"The best."

"We aren't the same two people. Those people were young and innocent."

"Yes, we've had to grow up in a way our parents didn't have to. But inside I'm still the same. I believe you are, too. Still full of dreams. Gentle. Kind."

"No. That man died back in France."

She nodded. He was partially right. He had changed. "The changes are simply layers that add maturity and depth."

"I wish I could believe you're right." He stared into the darkness and shuddered.

"I know I'm right." She laughed. "You'll have to trust me on this one."

Again he pulled himself back to her presence with visible effort and smiled, a smile so full of sweetness and sadness, her throat choked with tears. He stood, pulling her to her feet. "Come on then—let's go to bed."

☙

She awakened from her contented sleep. A flickering light danced across the floor at the foot of the bed. She reached out for Caleb, but his side of the bed was empty. "Caleb," she whispered, checking around the room, but she couldn't see him. She slipped from the bed to the doorway.

He reclined in the rocker, his head tilted back, low light shining from the lamp on the shelf next to him.

She watched him for a long time, seeing the gentle rise and fall of his chest, then took one of the quilts off the end of the bed and spread it over him. At her gentle touch, he flung out an arm, muttering something unintelligible. She ducked his arm and turned away, going back to the cold bed, where she lay shivering for a long time before sleep returned.

Caleb was up, the fire burning in the stove, when Lizzie hurried from the bedroom the next day. "Good morning," she called.

He nodded toward her. "It looks like a nice bright day."

"Did you sleep well?" She watched his reaction.

He slowly faced her. "Sometimes I can't sleep in the bed."

"Is there a particular reason?"

His gaze slid past her. His jaw tightened; then he shook his head. "It has nothing to do with you."

"Of course it does. I'm the one who wakes up with your side of the bed empty and wonders what's wrong."

His gaze flickered toward her. "Nothing's wrong."

"It seems to me there's plenty wrong when you huddle in a hard wooden chair all night long. And when you turn inward so often, it's like watching a revolving door. I can only guess at the reason." She paused to take a calming breath, praying for wisdom in the words she used. "But I don't mean to push you to talk about things you'd rather not. Just don't turn away from me."

Unblinking, he studied her several seconds. Slowly his shoulders relaxed, and he nodded. "Sorry if you worried about me last night."

She wiped at a smudge on the tabletop. He hadn't given any promises or offered any explanation, but something warned her not to push. He'd open up when the time was right. Meanwhile, she would do her best to show how much she loved him. And she'd pray for God's guidance and healing.

After he'd eaten, he pushed his chair back, his hands clenched in his lap. He shuffled his feet back and forth, then crossed one leg over the other and leaned back.

Lizzie, lingering over her tea, watched his fidgeting with curiosity.

Suddenly he dropped his chair to the floor and jerked to his feet. "I'm going for a walk."

She jumped up to ask if she could go with him, but he yanked his coat on and said, "I'm sure you'll be able to amuse yourself without me."

She sank back to the chair, rebuffed by his words. "I expect I can."

"I'll be back later." He jerked out the door.

She watched him through the window. Again he turned away from the farm, heading down the road. She sighed. It would take time for them to adjust. Although his welcome lacked a certain spark, at least he'd said he still loved her.

She hurried to the bedroom and pulled her Bible from her bag, then, sitting in the old rocker, opened it and read a chapter. It'd been hard to find a place and time for her usual Bible reading and prayer as they travelled, but now she was eager to reestablish her routine. She bowed her head and prayed, "God, things are not what I dreamed they'd be. Caleb seems so distant at times. Like he's forgotten I exist. In some ways it's been a bit of a disappointment, but at last I'm home. Caleb and I are together. Help me give my love unconditionally."

A knock on the door ended her prayers. "Come in," she called.

Mother Hughes pushed the door open. "I've brought you more eggs."

"Thank you." Lizzie took the basket. "I can't get over having so many eggs. Won't you come in?"

The older woman pulled out a chair. "Our hens lay good. I see to that. I give them boiled grain along with vegetable peelings. You treat hens right, and they'll reward you with plenty of eggs."

Lizzie nodded. "May I get you a cup of tea?"

"Tea would be fine."

Lizzie wished she had biscuits or cake to offer her mother-in-law and promised herself she would do some baking right away.

"I see you have some pictures up already."

"Paintings of home done by my younger sister."

Mother Hughes studied them for a moment. "Very nice."

"Would you like to see pictures of my family?" At a nod from the older woman, Lizzie hurried to the trunk to pull out her stack of photos. "These are my parents. Here's one of my sisters and me."

Mother Hughes nodded, sipping her tea as Lizzie talked about her home and family.

"Here are the three of us giving a concert in our parlor. We used to do that." She stopped, her throat tightening as she realized they would never be able to perform together again.

Mother Hughes suddenly pushed to her feet. "I have to get back to my work." She paused at the door. "Thank you for the tea."

Lizzie stared after her. She hadn't seen all the pictures. But she was right. There was work to be done. She'd unpack today. She lifted out the tray from the trunk. Her flute case lay cradled on the blankets. She pulled it out, her fingers lingering on the worn clasp; then she opened the case and folded back the blue velvet. Her fingers moving quickly, with practiced ease, she assembled her flute and began to play. The haunting strains of Mozart, Bach, and Beethoven filled her with sweet, gentle memories of home, even as her eyes flooded with tears. She ended with a piece Patricia had composed for them.

She carefully cleaned the instrument and put it away, humming as she pulled out one of the knitted patchwork blankets her grandma had made. Lizzie pressed the blanket to her face and breathed in the familiar smells of home, then draped it over the sofa.

By the time Caleb came stomping through the door, Lizzie

had placed photos along one shelf of the bookcase, stored her writing things on another shelf, and hung a quilt over the rocker to hide the peeling paint.

She turned from mixing a cake and smiled. "Hi."

"Smells good in here," Caleb said.

"I'm making a cake. Hope you like spice cake."

"I like any kind of cake." He looked around. "You've made the place look real nice."

"Thank you. I had a good morning. How about you?"

He nodded. "It was fine."

She poured the batter into pans and shoved them in the oven, muttering, "Now don't go flaring up and burn this." She gathered up the baking things, scraping a mouthful of batter into a spoon. "Want a taste?" She held it toward Caleb.

He tasted the batter and rolled his eyes, sighing his appreciation, before he pulled her to his lap and rubbed his nose against her cheek. "You'll spoil me."

"I'll do my best." She toyed with the curls behind his ear, her senses drowning in the nearness of him, the warmth of his arm around her waist, the illusive scent of sweat and spring.

He reached around her to scrape the bowl again. "Mmm. This is good."

She nuzzled his neck. "I like it, too."

He chuckled. "I don't think you mean the cake."

She giggled. "No, I don't." She wrapped her arms around his neck. The rasp of his whiskers sent delightful shivers along her nerves. "What do you do all day? I never saw you once."

"Nothing as fun as this. I was thinking about the first time I saw you."

"Umm. When Dad brought you home for tea. You walked in so tall and straight—"slender as a young sapling"—Dad said afterward, and stood looking around, your hat in your hand as if you didn't know whether to stay or hightail it while you could. I knew then if you stepped into the room, our lives would never be the same."

He shook his head. "That wasn't the first time I saw you."

"It wasn't?" But her attention was on the delicious warmth of his neck.

"I saw you earlier that day." His words were muffled against her hair.

"You never told me that." She settled into the crook of his arm. "Where did you see me?"

"The rest of the guys had gone to the pub. I wanted to get away from the racket, so I wandered up and down the streets. That's when I saw this beautiful girl skipping out of a shop. I moved closer to see her better. She had the prettiest hair, all shiny brown, and when she turned her head, it was like the sunshine reflected in her hair. And her face danced with joy. For a minute I couldn't even breathe. This gorgeous thing turned and waved to an older man and said, 'See you at tea, Dad,' and hurried down the street, where she joined two younger girls."

"That was me and my sisters?"

He stroked her hair. "It was. And I have a confession to make."

"Oh?"

"I followed you girls to the park. I couldn't help myself. You seemed to be having so much fun—laughing together like best friends. I watched you for a long time; then you went into a ladies' shop. I waited, but you didn't come out again."

"The Morrisons'. They have a flat in the back. We went in for tea."

"I waited until people started to stare. Then I headed back

for the shop where I first saw you. I don't know what I planned to do, but I walked in and looked around. I was surprised and pleased to see it was a bookstore. I was soon lost in looking through the old titles. I even found a book written by an explorer to Canada. Can you imagine reading about someone who was one of the first men to see the land where you now live?"

"Then what?"

"Then your father started talking to me, asking where I was from and about my family. I don't think it took him long to discover I was lonely and out of place. He took pity on me and asked me home for tea."

She felt him chuckle.

"I didn't have to be asked twice. I was sure I'd see you again." He hugged her. "I'm thankful I did."

She turned her head so she could see the smile on his face. "You never told me this before."

He smiled down at her. "When did I have time? You rushed me off my feet. Barely gave me time to make up my mind."

"Me? I remember it the other way around. Besides, I don't remember you protesting any at the time."

"I guess you wouldn't. Any more than you'll hear me protest now." He kissed her, driving away every thought but the taste of his lips and the way her heart swelled until she thought it would burst.

He lifted his head and sniffed appreciatively. "Something smells mighty fine. When will the cake be done?"

"Soon, if the stove cooperates."

He ran his finger around the rim of the mixing bowl and licked it. "Were you always such a good cook?"

She shook her head. "Mother and Patricia liked cooking so much that Vicky and I had to fight to get a chance." She laughed. "Not that we really cared. Both of us preferred housework, so I guess it was a good balance. But after you left, I made Mother promise to teach me everything when she could."

"I'd say if the cake is as good as the batter, you did all right."

"I've a few things yet to learn." She frowned at the big old stove. "For one thing, I'm determined to prove to this stubborn thing that I'm boss."

He grunted. "I always find a good hard kick works as a persuader."

"And here all I've done is stamp my foot." She giggled. "Maybe I need to be more forceful."

He sniffed again at the warm aroma coming from the oven. "How long did you say it would be? My mouth is watering for a big slice of cake right now."

Cocking her head to one side, she studied him playfully. "Why, Caleb Hughes—you know you can't have any cake until after your meal."

"Who says?" He grabbed her around the waist and waltzed her across the room, laughing. "Who says you can't have dessert first? Who says you have to take the bad with the good? Who says into each life some rain must fall?" He ground to a halt, staring into her face, his expression sobering. "Someone ought to write new rules."

A tremor shivered up her spine at the sudden change in him; a dark hollow look had replaced the sense of fun in his face. She grabbed his arm. "We can write new rules."

"It's too late," he muttered, returning to his chair, slumping over the table. "The old rules have already shaped our lives."

She stood beside him, placing her hand on his shoulder, feeling the tension in his muscles. "Our lives are not set in stone. God has redeemed us for His reasons. He's kindly seen us safely through the war. I'm certain He means for us to make the most of every opportunity that lies before us."

He flicked the spoon against his thumbnail, making a ticking sound. The fire crackled.

"My cake." She ran to pull it from the oven, setting the pans on the table to cool. "It looks about right." She was certain Mother and Patricia would have nodded approval. "Would you like some cake now?"

He shook his head. "I'll wait."

three

Next afternoon, Caleb headed down the road. Lizzie began to suspect it was a daily habit and promised herself she would ask him where he went and what he did for several hours every afternoon.

As she dried the last dish and put it away, a knock sounded. Before she could call out an answer, Mother Hughes entered with more eggs.

Lizzie hurried to take the basket. "If I can do anything to help with the chores, please let me know."

"Oh, no, my dear. I wouldn't let anyone interfere with my hens."

Lizzie laughed. "I have no intention of interfering. May I offer you a cup of tea?"

The older woman hesitated, then nodded and sat down. "I can't stay but a minute."

Lizzie made tea and cut a piece of cake.

Mother Hughes sipped her tea, then spoke. "I expect you find us quite different from what you're used to."

Lizzie smiled. "Not so as you'd notice."

"As time goes by, you'll find things we disagree on."

Lizzie studied the older woman. Dressed in black, her hair pulled back into a tight bun, she gave the impression of a small bird determined to get the worm. Lizzie's neck muscles tensed. "I hadn't planned on looking for things to disagree on. I plan to do my best to fit in."

Mother Hughes took another bite of cake before she resumed

her line of conversation. "No doubt you've been raised in a liberal home."

"I'm not sure what you mean." Lizzie kept her hands clasped together in her lap.

"For instance, the use of musical instruments. We believe God intended us to worship Him with our voices. Musical instruments are a worldly attraction. First Corinthians 14, verse 15, says, 'I will sing with the spirit, and I will sing with the understanding also.' Use of instruments only detracts from the spirit of worship and understanding." Mother Hughes kept her gaze on Lizzie as she lifted her cup to drink.

Lizzie stared at her, wondering why she felt compelled to tell her this. Suddenly an awful thought hit her. "My flute," she gasped. "You don't think I should play my flute." She swallowed hard, the very thought tearing at her heart.

"Would you mind, my dear? For our sake?"

Lizzie could only stare at her. How could she survive without her music? It had been her consolation since she was a young child. And somehow it bound her to her sisters. To give it up would be like ripping her family from her heart.

Mother Hughes was speaking again. "For Caleb, too. After all, it goes against his upbringing. I'm sure he would never say anything, but he must find it, well"—she seemed to search for the best word—"well, difficult."

A spear of pain shafted through Lizzie. She always thought Caleb took a great deal of pleasure from listening to her and her sisters play.

Somehow she managed to finish her tea and nod at the appropriate times as Mother Hughes talked about the weather. She managed to rise to her feet, disguising the way her limbs shook, and bid her mother-in-law a pleasant farewell; then she shut the door firmly and collapsed against it. Why hadn't Caleb told her this himself? Could she be so completely wrong about who he was?

She rushed to the trunk and pulled out her flute case, clutching it to her chest, rocking back and forth. She ached to find solace in playing but could not. She sobbed. Her family and all that was familiar and warm seemed to have been torn from her. Tears fell to her wrists, but she paid them no heed. After awhile, her tears spent, she pushed to her feet and retreated to the rocking chair. Taking her Bible, she read one of the psalms. " 'Praise Him for His mighty acts. . . . Praise Him with the sound of the trumpet: praise Him with psaltery and harp.' "

"Thank You for this message," she prayed. "I know it isn't wrong to love music. Not even the music made by instruments." But when would she ever get to satisfy her soul again?

She ached for her family, certain they would be missing her as much as she missed them, and pulled out her writing supplies to start a letter.

"Arrived safely. My new house is small." A picture would tell far more than she could hope to convey with words, so she picked up her colored pencils and sketched a drawing of the house. She had to slip outside several times to get the details fixed in her mind correctly—the color of the spindly trees showing the first signs of new growth, the size of the dark evergreens standing guard along the edge of the yard, the bulk of the red barn, the green-trimmed white house set to the right of her own little place.

"Caleb's parents are—" She hesitated, not wanting to paint a picture tainted by her recent pain. "His mother is small, birdlike. His father is quiet and seems gentle." With quick, deft strokes, she drew a black-and-white picture of her in-laws—Mother Hughes in black from neck to ankle like a crow; Father Hughes at her side, leaning against a rake.

She held the picture at arm's length and smiled. She was no artist like Vicky, although she'd always been able to do people better, but the simple sketches accurately portrayed the older couple. She peered at the drawing more closely, trying to ascertain if she had given away more than she planned with the tight-lipped expression on Mother Hughes's face, but decided it was not an unkind expression.

"Caleb is well, though very thin." Again a few quick strokes and she had Caleb's likeness. She liked it so well, she did another to keep.

"I have not been any farther than across the yard to meet the in-laws," she penned. "Perhaps tomorrow I will go for a walk. The weather is pleasantly warm. I think I'll see if I can discover any wildflowers."

She folded the pages and slipped them into an envelope. When Caleb came home, she'd ask him about mailing the letter.

🙠

He lay beside her in bed, the lamp burning low.

"Caleb, your mother was over to visit. Actually she's been every day to bring more eggs."

"Uh-huh."

"She said your beliefs teach the use of musical instruments is wrong." She gulped, surprised at how much it hurt just to say the words aloud.

"That's what they teach." He sounded groggy. Lizzie found it strange that he could seem so uninterested.

"Do you agree?"

"Not really."

Her breath whooshed out of her. "I didn't think you could."

"Mother and Dad believe in leading sober lives."

Lizzie nodded, remembering the verse on the wall in her mother-in-law's kitchen.

"We never played games. Fact is, I can't remember hardly ever laughing without being admonished to restrain myself." He shrugged, his warm arm rubbing against her.

"Sounds dreadful."

"I never thought much about it. Guess I thought every family was like that until I met yours."

She giggled. "We must have seemed very frivolous."

He chuckled. She turned her head, pressing her ear against his side, enjoying the rumbling sound in his chest. "I didn't know what to think at first. But it didn't take me long to realize what I'd been missing."

"We had some good times, didn't we?"

He kissed the top of her head. "The best." He loosened his arms so he could look into her face. "Aren't you going to miss all that?"

She turned to meet his gaze, hanging on to the warmth there. Tonight he seemed to have lost the dark spells that came over him occasionally. She drew her fingers along his lips. "Your mother asked me not to play my flute." She tried to keep her voice light but knew her pain drew her words tight.

He crushed her to his chest. "Lizzie. I'm sorry. I don't suppose you could play it quietly?"

"A flute?" The idea so tickled her that she giggled.

He chuckled. "I guess not."

Smiling now, she asked, "Could I play it somewhere else?"

"Like where?"

"I don't know. Maybe I could walk down the road a ways."

"I don't see why not."

"That's what I'll do then." But talk about going down the road brought another thought to her mind. "Where do you go every day when you go down the road?"

He grew very still.

"I'm not meaning to pry."

"You're not prying. It's just something I don't talk about much."

"I understand." But even as she told herself he was entitled to his own life, a trickle of hurt made her desperate to know.

"I have a friend in town."

She waited, wondering if the friend was male or female.

"Frankie Duncan."

She scolded herself for her doubts.

"We signed up together."

"You must share a lot of memories."

He shifted away, freeing his arm from around her shoulders, and crossed his hands across his chest. "Too many." She could feel the tension in him.

"Could I go with you to visit Frankie?"

He was quiet so long, she thought he wasn't going to give her an answer; then, his voice strained, he said, "I'll ask."

She curled against him, trying to get him to return to their former closeness, but he remained stiff at her side. She relaxed, willing herself to sleep. A few minutes later, he slipped out of bed and left the room. What troubled him so much as to drive him from his bed—and from her arms—every night?

❧

The next afternoon, remembering Caleb's assurance she could play her flute away from the yard, Lizzie waited until Mother Hughes had delivered the eggs and had shared a hurried cup of tea before she headed down the road.

It was the first time she'd had a chance to be away from the farm, and the open spaces, with so little sign of human habitation, enthralled her. The road dipped between a stand of tall, almost green poplars; and she turned aside, breathing deeply of the pungent poplar smell. In sunny spots the grass grew verdant and fresh. Spring, her favorite time of year with its riotous growth and untamed colors.

She found a sunny spot and began to play, letting the haunting strains of her music drift along the hills and waltz through the trees.

A young lad, about ten or eleven, slid into view. He crouched down on his legs and listened with rapt attention.

She lowered her instrument. "Hello. What's your name?"

"Robbie."

"My name is Lizzie. Do you like my playing?"

He nodded, his eyes sparkling. "I never heard nothing like it before. What do you call that thing?"

"It's a flute. A woodwind instrument."

"It sounds lonesome." He shifted closer.

"It makes happy, dancing sounds, too. Like this." She played him a lively tune.

He clapped his hands. "I like that," he said when she finished. "Is it hard to play?"

"Would you like to try?"

He reached out eagerly. "Can I?"

She showed him how to hold it and blow across the mouthpiece. He looked surprised when no sound came out. "You have to concentrate your breath," she explained.

He tried again, grinning when he produced an uncertain note, then handed the flute back to her. "Play some more."

She played a march, then lowered the instrument. "I suppose you live close by."

He nodded. "Over the hill on the edge of town." He studied her. "You new here, ain't ya?"

She nodded. "Only been here a few days."

"Say, I bet you're Caleb's wife. He said you were somethin' special."

Pleased at the comment, she grinned at him. "He did, did he? I'm taking it you must know him well."

The boy nodded, his eyes serious. "Pretty good, I guess, though it's really my dad he comes to see. Say, could you come and play for my dad? He'd like it some, I bet. Please, lady—Mrs. Hughes."

His intensity touched her as much as his obvious closeness to Caleb. "You say it isn't far?"

"Oh, no. Just a hop, skip, and a jump away. You'll come then?"

She nodded. "If you're sure it's all right. Your mother won't mind?"

"She'd think it grand." He ran toward the road. "Come on—I'll show you the way."

"Wait while I get my flute."

He danced from foot to foot as he waited for her to fall in step with him. She could feel him urging her to greater haste as they hurried toward town.

"See—that's our place." He pointed to a narrow, two-storied house surrounded by a tall hedge.

"It looks big." Not only the house but also the wide barn beside it.

"Yup. My dad built the place with room to grow. He owns the freight company, you know." He slowed slightly. " 'Course he can't work now."

Before Lizzie could ask why his father no longer worked, the boy drew her up the path toward the house. He rushed through the door calling, "Ma, I brought somebody to meet you." Then remembering his manners, he came back to Lizzie. "Come on in."

"Child, what's all the racket about?" A plump lady with a tangle of auburn hair hurried into the room. "Oh, I beg yer pardon. I didn't realize we had visitors."

"Ma, this is Mrs. Caleb. I mean Mrs. Hughes. Caleb's wife. Her name's Lizzie."

The woman wiped her hands on her apron, then engulfed Lizzie's hands in both hers. "I say welcome. Glad I am to make your acquaintance. By the way, I'm Pearl Duncan."

"Duncan?" Lizzie wondered why the name should be familiar.

"Ma, she can play the flute real purty. I asked her if she would play for Dad, and she said she would."

"Well, now, isn't that grand? But let's not be forgetting our manners." She took Lizzie's hand and led her toward a big table with golden loaves of bread cooling on a towel. "I'm thinking ye'd be liking a spot of tea." She turned to Robbie. "You run and tell your dad we have company." Lizzie didn't catch the rest of what she said to the boy before Robbie dashed through an open door into another room.

"Tea would be nice." Lizzie took the chair indicated and looked around. Two little heads peeked at her from behind another chair.

"Come on, you two. Say hello to Mrs. Hughes—Caleb's wife."

A boy and a girl slid into sight. "This is Violet." She indicated the little girl with sober, brown eyes. "She's eight. And this"—she pulled the tiny, frightened boy forward—"is Junior. He's almost five now."

Lizzie said hello to the shy pair.

"Children, say hello."

The two mumbled a response and ducked out of sight.

Pearl set a cup in front of Lizzie, studying her openly. "Caleb has told us a lot about you."

That surprised Lizzie. He must tell these people more than

he did her. "Is he here now?"

Pearl nodded. "Comes every day, but of course you know that. Say, how are you liking your new home? Caleb said it was a pretty poor offering." The woman stirred a generous spoonful of sugar into her tea.

"I'm liking it fine." Lizzie felt slightly bewildered by the disadvantage this woman had over her—she seemed to know a great deal about Lizzie, whereas Lizzie knew nothing of her.

"I assured him you would be so glad to see him you wouldn't mind at all where you lived."

Lizzie laughed. "I told him the same thing myself."

"There now. Don't I always say women have a way of knowing?" Her expression grew thoughtful. "I don't know what we'd do without Caleb's help."

Having no idea what the woman meant, Lizzie nodded.

"Lizzie. What are you doing here?"

Startled by Caleb's voice, she jerked around to face him. "Robbie brought me—I hope you don't mind."

Pearl rose and took her teacup. "Come along then and meet Frankie. He'll be pleased finally to lay eyes on you."

Lizzie looked from her husband to the woman and back again. Frankie? Suddenly she understood. This was Frankie Duncan's home—the place Caleb visited every day. Her senses sharpened, and she studied Pearl more closely. No longer young, the woman still bore the marks of beauty with her bright hair and dark brown eyes.

"Bring your tea," Pearl ordered, leading the way into the other room.

Lizzie hesitated. Was Caleb reluctant to share this corner of his life with her? But Pearl's urging drove them forward into the next room.

At once she saw the man lying on a bed against the far

wall, some sort of contraption holding the covers off his feet. A glance told her this was the hub of the home. Chairs clustered around the bed; books, games, and used plates proclaimed family life centered here.

"Bring her closer," the man called.

Pearl waved her forward.

Lizzie set her teacup on a side table and stepped toward the man.

"Frankie dear, this is Lizzie, Caleb's wife." Pearl smiled as she turned to Lizzie. "I'd like you to meet my husband, Frankie."

Lizzie looked into his face and met a pair of bright blue eyes, twinkling with pleasure. "So I finally get to meet the sweet lass that has occupied this young fellow's thoughts for so long." He took her hand between his. " 'Tis my pleasure. I hope I'll see a great deal more of you."

Her heart immediately warmed. "I'm certain you shall."

"I'm grateful for yer good husband's help. He does his best to see that I'm kept amused. Here, have a look at Petey." He pointed to a wire cage on the shelf at his side.

Lizzie leaned forward. At first she didn't see anything; then Frankie tweaked the wire and made a kissing noise. A fat brown mouse stirred from a nest of torn paper and ambled toward Frankie's finger.

Lizzie jerked back. "A mouse."

Frankie laughed. Behind her, Pearl and Caleb chuckled, and the children giggled.

"This is a special mouse. Lizzie, meet Petey." The mouse sniffed Frankie's finger, then shuffled away to scratch at a pile of seeds. "You see—Caleb caught this mouse and tamed him for me. Me and Petey have a good time. I could bring him out and let you hold him." His eyes twinkled.

Lizzie shuddered. "No, thanks." The children giggled again.

Little Violet sidled up to her father. "Could I hold him, Daddy?"

"You climb up here beside me, and you can hold him for a bit."

Pearl lifted the child to the bed, setting her carefully at Frankie's side, then lowered the cage to Frankie's chest. He unwired a gate and scooped up the mouse, handing it to Violet, who cupped her hands and held the animal close to her chest. Frankie stroked the child's head a moment, then turned back to Lizzie, his eyes glistening.

"I am so fortunate to be surrounded by friends and family."

Lizzie's nose stung with tears, but she managed to keep her voice clear. "I hope you'll count me among your friends." Something about this man and his family touched a tender spot in her heart.

"Why, my dear, I feel I've known you for years." He grinned suddenly and turned to Caleb. "She's every bit as pretty as you said."

"I already told her that." It was Pearl. She sat in a chair close to Frankie's head. "Pull up a chair," she told Lizzie.

But Caleb had already drawn two chairs close and held one for Lizzie before he plopped down on the other.

The younger boy—Junior—leaned against his mother's knee, but Robbie opted for sitting cross-legged on the floor at Caleb's side.

"It was me who found her," Robbie pointed out. "I heard her playing a"—he turned to Lizzie—"a flute, right?"

Lizzie nodded, enjoying herself thoroughly. This was how she remembered family life—sharing and playing, a sense of closeness.

"She plays real good. I made her promise she'd play for you, Dad."

A tightness crossed Frankie's face, and then he smiled. "I'd like that, Lizzie. Will you play for us now?"

"Of course."

Robbie shot out of the room, returning immediately with her flute.

Remembering Mother Hughes's opinion, she asked, "Are you sure you want to hear me?"

Pearl leaned forward eagerly. "Would be our pleasure."

Lizzie turned to Caleb, and when he nodded encouragement, she lifted her flute and began to play some lively tunes.

Pearl leaned back, smiling.

Frankie stared at the ceiling, a contented look on his face.

Little Violet's eyes grew round as saucers.

The little boy, Junior, edged away from his mother and began swaying in time to the music.

Lizzie stopped playing, fearing she would bore them. She dropped her gaze to Robbie. He grinned widely and murmured, "I knew they'd like it."

" 'Tis the music I've been dreaming of for months," Frankie said. He reached out and squeezed Lizzie's hand. "Thank you. You're a fine gal." He lay back. "Would you mind giving us another tune?"

Violet dropped the mouse back in its cage and scrambled from the bed.

Lizzie was certain she heard Frankie groan and shot a worried look at Caleb. He nodded. She took her flute again and played while her heart unfolded with the warmth of this family and the encouragement of Caleb's steady gaze.

Violet took Junior's hand, and together they twirled and pirouetted to the music.

four

Lizzie lowered the flute and waited as the strains of the music drifted away.

Frankie coughed and flinched.

"Come on, children." Pearl sprang to her feet. "Your dad needs his rest."

Lizzie cleaned the flute and folded it away. "I've overstayed my welcome."

"Not at all," Pearl reassured her. "It's been a pleasure."

"You'll come again?" Frankie sounded tired, but he reached for her hand, holding it insistently until she promised to return.

The sound of a heavy wagon rumbled past the house. Pearl cocked her head to listen. "That's Audie. Robbie, run out and give him a hand."

Robbie called good-bye to Lizzie and Caleb before he raced out the door.

Caleb took the flute case. "See you tomorrow," he murmured to Pearl, then turned to Lizzie. "I'll see you home."

As they stepped into the sunshine, she fingered the fat envelope in her pocket. "Can I mail a letter someplace?"

"I'll show you the post office." They turned down the long wide street. From the barn came the noise of harnesses rattling and horses blowing. She caught the sound of Robbie's voice and a deeper, slower one answering.

"Frankie owns a delivery business," Caleb explained. "He left Pearl and his driver, Audie, to run it while he was away at war. I don't know what he'll do now. He can't run a wagon anymore. It's a shame—the thriving business would be a good source of income for the family."

"How long before he's up and about again?"

Caleb's steps slowed. "He's not going to get better."

Lizzie gasped and stopped to stare at him. "He's dying?"

Caleb nodded, his face a blanket of despair. "Pearl insisted on bringing him home from the hospital. Said she wanted to care for him." He dragged his fingers through his hair, tangling his curls.

"What's the matter with him?"

Caleb's eyes darkened, his expression hardened. "He's suffering the glories of war. Trench foot. Lungs damaged by chlorine gas." He kicked a rock down the road. "And that's the least of it."

She'd heard of trench foot—where the feet rotted because of standing in water-soaked boots day after day. Her heart felt heavy, lifeless. "But he seems so cheerful. So does Pearl."

He nodded. "Guess they keep up their spirits for the children." He kicked again, leaving a pockmark in the dirt. "It shouldn't be Frankie."

The way he said it troubled Lizzie in a way she couldn't understand. "It shouldn't happen to anyone," she corrected.

He stomped on down the road, Lizzie hurrying to keep pace. He didn't slow until he pulled abreast of a square brick structure. "Here we are."

"I'll only be a moment," she called, hurrying inside. The blond young woman behind the wicket took the envelope and studied it carefully.

"You'd be the new Mrs. Hughes."

"Yes."

"Why did you Brits have to steal our men away? Weren't there enough on your side of the ocean without taking ours?"

Lizzie drew back. "We didn't ask for war any more than you did."

"Mr. Hughes already picked up the mail." The girl turned away, ending the conversation.

Lizzie fled out the door.

Caleb stood looking in the window of the store next door. At her approach, he turned away, heading out of town without a glance in her direction.

She choked back her confusion. Nothing seemed quite as she had imagined it would. She pushed her shoulders back. She had to give things time.

&

"We'll go with my parents," Caleb announced, waiting at the door for her to join him for church.

Her enthusiasm dampened at the sight of her in-laws, stiff and straight on the buggy seat, but she nodded and joined Caleb and accepted his help to the seat behind Mother Hughes.

"Good morning," she greeted them.

"Good morning, Elizabeth." Father Hughes smiled over his shoulder, then flicked the reins.

"It's a fine Sabbath day," Mother Hughes said. "A day holy unto the Lord."

Her anticipation returning, Lizzie smiled at Caleb. She loved church—the singing, the way the light shafted through the windows touching this one or that in blessing, the soft rustle as everyone rose or sat in unison.

Caleb squeezed her hand. Content, she settled back for the ride into town.

Only they didn't turn toward town; they turned in the opposite direction. She shot Caleb a questioning look, but he sat back, staring straight ahead. She had assumed church was in Silver Creek, but perhaps there were other towns around, or the church might even be on a quiet little plot of land away from town. Her puzzlement returned, however, when Father Hughes turned toward a low, white house. Several buggies and one wagon stood before the house.

"I understood we were going to church," she murmured, turning toward Caleb, but it was Mother Hughes who answered.

"We meet in homes as the New Testament church did."

"I see." The building made little difference; it was the people and the singing and the reading of Scripture that cheered and blessed.

Holding Caleb's hand, she followed his parents inside. As she glanced around, her heart plummeted to her feet. Everyone sat in a circle, eyes darting toward the newcomers for an instant, then returning to quiet contemplation of the floor. But what made her feel as conspicuous as a squalling baby was that all the women wore black dresses to their ankles; all wore black scarves over their heads.

Lizzie held back, acutely aware of the brightness of her dark blue dress, which seemed obscenely short in the midst of these sober people. "I don't belong here," she whispered to Caleb past the constriction in her throat.

He squeezed her hand and drew her to the pair of empty chairs next to the door. Lizzie sat down, heat rushing up her cheeks. Her head lowered, she allowed herself a quick glance around the circle. An older couple sat across the room from her. To her right were a younger couple and three children at their side. The children sat still as statues. The youngest, a boy of about six or seven, squirmed. His father touched the boy's shoulder, and the lad stiffened. Lizzie glanced over the others and blinked as she encountered a pair of bright eyes. The girl across the room smiled before she ducked her head.

"Could we sing number seventy-eight?"

Lizzie jerked her head to see who spoke. It was one of the older men who remained seated. Suddenly little black hymnals appeared in each hand. Caleb held one toward her.

Then, without any instruments, the group sang. Lizzie choked back the sadness tearing at her throat as she listened to the mournful tones of the group. Singing, she guessed from their demeanor, was not meant to be enjoyed.

After five stanzas, the song ended, and silence again descended on the room.

"I'd like to share from 1 Thessalonians chapter 5." A grayhaired portly man opened his Bible, waiting for the rest to find the place. Lizzie found the passage in her Bible; then she and Caleb bent over the pages as the older man read.

" 'Let us watch and be sober.' A timely admonition for us, I believe." The older man went on to warn the others to be constantly watching for Christ's return and to be on guard against Satan's wily attacks. "Let us pray." The prayer continued for what seemed to Lizzie a very long time. Her head drooped, and she jerked forward as waves of sleep swirled around her. It was the longest prayer she'd ever heard. It amazed her that the little ones across the room could be still so long.

Finally the man uttered, "Amen." But the assembly remained seated, their heads bowed.

Her legs began to ache. She shifted ever so slightly and was certain every pair of eyes turned toward her.

Someone called out another hymn number. They sang six droning verses. Another man prayed for almost as long as the first. Another hymn was called out; then some unseen signal announced it was over. There was a general rustle as people rose, murmured quiet greetings, and filed outside.

Caleb introduced her to the others as they made their way to the buggy. The only name Lizzie could focus on was that of a young woman—Molly something or other—who leaned closer and said, "I'm so pleased to meet you. I've longed to see another young woman in that room."

Lizzie met the girl's eyes and saw a flash of humor. "Glad to meet you," she said. She looked down at her skirt and grimaced. "It seems black is the only appropriate color. I wish I'd known."

Molly patted her hand. "I'd wear bright colors if it weren't for my father." She nodded toward a tall, heavyset man. "He thinks I should look and act like an old woman." Molly's eyes flashed. "But I want to be young first."

Lizzie grinned, liking this girl. "Where do you live?"

Molly pointed to the south. "A couple of miles that way."

Lizzie bit her bottom lip. It would be several miles from where she and Caleb lived. What a disappointment. She sensed Molly would make a good friend. "I wish you would come and visit me."

Molly's gaze darted to her father, then back to Lizzie. "I just might do that."

Caleb turned from speaking to the father of three children. "Mother and Dad are waiting," he said to Lizzie then. "See you later, Molly."

❧

The buggy turned into the yard, but Father Hughes did not stop at the little house. Instead he drove on to the bigger house before he reined in the horses.

"I have dinner ready," Mother Hughes called over her shoulder. "Didn't think there was much point in both of us making a meal."

Lizzie shot Caleb a startled look.

"Do you mind?" he asked, low enough so his mother wouldn't hear.

She shrugged. She longed to have Caleb to herself and ask him the questions filling her mind. On the other hand, it would be nice to sit down to someone else's cooking. "Thank you," she said to her mother-in-law.

Inside, a cloth lay over the table. Mother Hughes lifted it off carefully. The table was fully set, with biscuits piled on a plate. The older woman removed saucers covering several small bowls. Pink pickled beets, green dills, and bread-and-butter pickles filled the air with spicy, sharp smells. A bowl of bright red canned tomatoes sat in the center of the table.

Mother Hughes disappeared into the pantry and returned with a plate of sliced meat.

"You've gone to a lot of work," Lizzie said.

"I did it last night," Mother Hughes said, indicating the others should sit at the table. "We don't work on the Sabbath."

Lizzie felt reprimanded; yet the idea of not having to do any sort of work for one day held vast appeal. "Not anything?"

Father Hughes chuckled. "The cow must be milked, of course. And in the winter, the fires must be fed."

Mother Hughes nodded. "But in the summer we don't light a fire. We do what is essential." She gave Lizzie a sweet smile. "I expect you find our ways different. I hope you can get used to them."

"I expect I can do about anything I put my mind to doing." She hadn't meant to sound so sharp, but Mother Hughes had a way of phrasing her words to make it seem as if she doubted Lizzie could adjust to her new life.

"I wouldn't be too prideful if I were you," Mother Hughes warned, softening her words with a gentle tone and a soft smile. " 'Pride goeth before destruction.' "

Lizzie laughed, though the words stung. "I'm not meaning to be prideful. I know I'll make more than my share of mistakes, especially if I don't know what's expected." She paused, letting both Caleb and Mother Hughes feel the weight of accusation in her words. Either one of them could have warned her of their beliefs instead of springing things on her out of the blue. "But I hope I learn from my mistakes."

Father Hughes interrupted before anyone could respond. "Why don't I ask the blessing so we can eat?"

&

She waited until they were alone in their own home before she turned to Caleb. "Why didn't you tell me I should wear black to church?"

He cocked his head and studied her. "Because I like you in that dress. It suits you."

She blinked. It was hard to remain annoyed at a man who gave her compliments. "Thank you, but don't you see how uncomfortable it made me?" And how it gave her mother-in-law more things to criticize. "I don't know what's expected if you don't tell me. Everything is so different."

"I guess I didn't say anything because it truly doesn't matter to me."

"But all those other people. What do you think they thought?"

Again he shrugged. "It doesn't matter what they think. Besides, I expect most of those women would like to have a dress like yours."

Lizzie was mystified. "Then why don't they? Why do they wear black if they don't like it?"

Caleb sighed. "Because the church teaches the women are to be in subjection to the men. And the deacons say a modest woman will wear black." He scrubbed a hand through his hair.

The whole idea seemed strange to her. "My mother obeys

my father, but she's allowed to choose her own clothes."

"I'm not agreeing with the way they do things. In fact, I'm half convinced most of the men would rather like to see their womenfolk in something besides black."

She spread her hands. "Then why—"

"I think everyone is afraid they'll be accused of not being sober and vigilant if they change anything."

Lizzie thought of the verse hanging prominently on her in-laws' kitchen wall. "But what about the joy of the Lord, the joy of His salvation?" His expression grew troubled. "Caleb, what do you believe?"

He shook his head. "I'm not sure. I don't necessarily agree with my parents, but on the other hand, how much joy do we deserve? It seems you do your best, but it isn't nearly good enough, and then you die."

"Caleb." His words sent shock waves through her body. "Sounds to me like a you're-born, you-suffer, you-die fatalistic approach to life." She crossed her arms over her chest as if she could block the dark thoughts from her heart. "I don't believe life is like that at all, and I can't believe the Caleb I had so many fun times with in England is saying it. You used to reach out for life with an eagerness that made me laugh with joy. You wanted to see and touch and taste everything so long as it wasn't sinful."

"That Caleb died in France." He turned away to stare out the window.

She stood looking at him, hearing his words but wondering if she'd misunderstood them. A shudder snaked up her spine and rattled her jaw. She pulled her thoughts together. "I don't believe that," she whispered. "I've seen glimpses of the old Caleb."

He kept his eyes turned toward the window. "I will never

be the old Caleb again."

"I suppose not. But you'll be a better, stronger man instead." She didn't dare contemplate any other option.

Still staring out the window, he didn't answer. "There's a storm brewing," he muttered. "It must have slipped in from the north."

"Caleb?" She touched his arm, wanting to continue their discussion, but he jolted away as if he'd been struck.

Lizzie pulled her hand back, pressing it to her stomach. He'd never flinched from her touch before. Maybe he had changed more than she guessed. A chill settled into her bones.

Lightning flashed in the distance. Thunder rumbled.

Caleb shuddered. "I hope it misses us."

Lizzie stared at his back.

The storm grew closer, the lightning brighter. Thunder rumbled and rattled. Then rain slashed against the window.

Caleb spun away from the window. He huddled on the rocker, pulling the quilt around his shoulders. Leaning over his knees, he cradled his head in his hands. "I hate rain," he muttered. "Rain and mud and thunder." He moaned—a sound that drove fear into Lizzie's heart. What had happened to her bright young husband? He seemed to have disappeared inside the body of someone she didn't know or understand.

"Caleb, it's only a shower." She stood at his side, longing to wrap her arms around him and comfort him. As if reading her thoughts, he stiffened and turned his shoulder to her. She didn't dare touch him for fear of being pushed away.

A plopping sound pulled her attention away from Caleb.

"A leak," she cried and hurried to put a bowl on the table to catch the drip. Another plop. This time by the bookcase. "My pictures." She swept them into her arms and, looking around for a safe place, opened the trunk and tossed them in, hurrying to put out another bowl. By the time the shower ended, she had a half dozen bowls and pans set out to catch drips and had rescued Granny's blanket and a stack of books.

Throughout the storm, Caleb remained huddled in the rocker, shuddering at every clap of thunder.

The storm passed. The thunder ended. The rain stopped. The drips slowed. Still Caleb sat with his legs drawn close to his chest, his head bowed.

"Caleb?" Lizzie moved closer. "The storm is over."

He nodded. Slowly, as if it required an effort, he pulled himself upright, his hands clenched into tight fists in his lap. A shudder shook his shoulders.

five

Disregarding Mother Hughes's instructions not to light a fire, Lizzie soon had a hearty blaze going in the stove. She made a pot of tea and carried a cupful to Caleb.

His eyes had a faraway look in them. She wondered if he even saw her as he took the cup and slowly sipped the contents while she sat on the edge of the sofa, close to his knees.

After a moment, his eyes focused, and he turned toward her. "Sorry about that. I hate storms."

She nodded, waiting for him to explain his reaction.

He took a long drink, then muttered, "I hate rain." Suddenly he pushed to his feet, set the cup on the table, and stomped from the house.

Lizzie stared after him. "Now what?" she muttered. But no explanation awaited her, and she set about gathering up the pots and bowls, pitching the water outside. She was washing and drying them when she heard a sound on the roof and rushed outside to see Caleb with a bundle of shingles and a handful of nails climbing a ladder to the roof.

Seeing her, he called, "I'll fix those leaks. No need to have rain inside as well as out."

For a moment she watched, then turned back inside, relieved he seemed to be back to normal. Hammering rattled overhead.

"Caleb?" Father Hughes's voice reached her from outside the house.

She wiped her hands and went to join the older man.

"What's he doing?" Father Hughes asked.

"Fixing the roof. It leaked in several places."

"Caleb?" his father called again, louder this time.

Caleb stopped hammering and turned to peer at the two below him. "Hi."

"Have you forgotten it's the Lord's Day?"

Caleb shook his head. "Nope."

"We don't work on the Lord's Day," his father reminded him gently.

"The good Lord saw fit to send rain on the Sabbath so I'm thinking He was reminding me the roof needs repairs." Caleb turned back to place a nail and pound it in.

"Your mother is upset at listening to hammering."

"I'm sorry."

Lizzie didn't think he sounded a bit sorry, and as if to prove her correct, he pounded in another nail.

"Caleb?" His father's voice grew firmer.

But Caleb only pounded in another nail.

Lizzie edged back, not wanting to get involved. Quietly, before either man could say something to her, she slipped inside and soundlessly closed the door, through which she could still hear the conversation.

"Caleb, will you honor our wishes?" his father persisted.

The hammering continued without interruption.

She waited, barely breathing. When she heard no more voices, she stole a peek out the window and saw Father Hughes tramping back to the house. She sank into a chair, pressing the heels of her hands into her eyes. What did it mean? What drove Caleb to defy his parents? Who was this man she had married?

Caleb worked on the roof the rest of the afternoon, finally coming down for supper. He went back outside almost before he'd finished eating. As she washed dishes, she saw him go to the barn and return with a bucket and a hammer. He eyed the barn, then walked the fence line.

That night he crawled into bed beside her and pulled her into his arms. "I see a hundred different things around the place that need fixing."

"You sound happy about it."

He chuckled, and she snuggled close, lulled by the rumble of his voice and the beat of his heart.

"Just happy that I can fix them."

He fell asleep almost at once. She stayed cuddled in his arms, rejoicing that the old Caleb had returned. The one who had sat huddled and shivering on the rocker was a stranger—a frightening stranger.

When she awoke the next morning, Caleb was gone. She heard hammering and jumped from bed to race to the window. In the pink early morning light, he sat high atop the barn, poking in new shingles and hammering them in place. Shaking her head and smiling, she got dressed and prepared breakfast, then went out to the barn. "Caleb," she called. "Breakfast is ready."

He jerked in her direction, a startled look on his face, and then a slow smile softened the dark planes. "I'll be right down." He shuffled across the sharply sloped roof as Lizzie held her breath, fearing he would fall. He climbed down the ladder and came to her side.

"Thought I'd get an early start." He leaned back, his hands in his rear pockets, looking pleased with himself.

"You must have been up before the birds."

"Nope. They were scolding and cleaning house when I got the ladder." He dropped his arm over Lizzie's shoulder and turned her toward their home.

By noon, when he quit to eat, the barn roof was splattered with new shingles.

Mother Hughes came over with the eggs before Caleb left. "It's nice to see you work, Son."

Lizzie blinked. The older woman made it sound like Caleb's working was an unexpected bonus. Lizzie kept a firm rein on her tongue to keep from leaping to Caleb's defense.

Caleb only leaned back in his chair and smiled—a smile, Lizzie noted, that did not reach his eyes. "I've always worked, Mother."

"Before you left us to go overseas, I guess you did."

Lizzie gave the woman tea and gulped hurriedly from her own cup. "That little rain certainly freshened the air," she said.

"Rain this time of year is good," Mother Hughes agreed, then turned to smile at Caleb. "Did you forget the command to rest on the Sabbath?"

Caleb tilted his chair back so far, Lizzie feared he would end up on his head. He locked his hands behind his neck before he answered. "I didn't forget."

His mother shook her head. "But I heard you—saw you—repairing the roof yesterday. The Sabbath, I might remind you."

Caleb nodded. "Like I told Dad, the good Lord saw fit to send rain on the Sabbath. I figured He was telling me it was time to fix the leaks."

Mother Hughes drew her mouth tight. "I'm certain He meant no such thing." Her eyes narrowed. "But what can I expect? I'm sure you encountered all sorts of temptations and heathenism over there." Her gaze lingered on Lizzie.

Lizzie's fingers dug into her palms. She stared into her tea. It was obvious her mother-in-law held Lizzie responsible for Caleb's choices. An unfair assessment. Lizzie had nothing to do with it.

Caleb dropped his chair with a thud. "I certainly did, and if it weren't for Lizzie and her family befriending me, I don't know where I might have ended. They're a fine Christian family who showed me nothing but charity." He jerked to his feet. "Life doesn't always fit into neat little slots, Mother." He stomped out the door.

Lizzie held her breath as the door slammed behind him. She darted a cautious look at her mother-in-law and saw a flash of pain cross the older woman's face. She understood how difficult it must be to see her son slipping away from her, and Lizzie's heart went out to the woman. She covered Mother Hughes's hand with her own. "He didn't mean to hurt you. It's just that it's hard for him to fit back in after being at war."

Mother Hughes blinked hard, then moved her hands to her lap. "It's more than that. He's changed. He's not the boy he used to be."

"No, he's now a man."

Mother Hughes gave her a strained look, as if the thought of her boy becoming a man was more than she could bear. "Thank you again for the tea. I'm sure you have as much to do as I."

Lizzie watched her go, wishing she could find a common ground with this woman. But, despite their shared love for Caleb, Lizzie felt like an ocean separated them—an ocean as vast and wide as the Atlantic she had recently crossed.

She had no doubt as to where Caleb had gone and stared down the road, wishing she could have gone with him to visit the Duncans. Her house felt stifling. She grabbed her flute case and headed in the same direction as before and, standing under the same tree, began to play. After several songs, she glanced up to see Robbie watching from a nearby rock.

"Hi," she called. "I didn't hear you come."

"I was quiet." He grinned. "Besides, you had your eyes closed."

"I did?" She tried to look startled but ended up laughing. Patricia and Vicky always teased her that they could tell she was sad because she shut her eyes to play the flute. "I guess I get lost in my music."

"It's nice. I like it."

"Thank you." She sat on a log beside him. "How are you today?"

"Oh. All right." He shrugged.

"You don't sound very sure. Want to talk about it?"

He looked at her, his blue eyes—so much like his father's—troubled. "Do you ever get mad about the war?"

"I guess I do. It turned most people's lives upside down. It seems impossible to get it back right."

"Yeah. That's what I mean." He pulled a blade of grass and chewed the tender end. "Nothing will ever be the same again."

She sat beside him, sharing his sadness. "I guess what we have to do is concentrate on what's left rather than what's gone."

"I worry about my dad." The boy kept his face averted, as if trying to hide his emotions.

Lizzie wasn't sure how to respond. How much did this boy know or suspect of his father's condition?

Robbie jerked about to face her, his eyes brimming with emotion. "Why does my dad have to put up with so much?"

"I can't answer that." Tears stung her eyes. "Life is full of things I have no answer for."

He threw the blade of grass with a vengeance. "It doesn't make sense."

They sat silently for a moment. Lizzie wished she had an

answer for this child's torment. Finally she drew a long, shaky breath. "You could get lost in trying to sort out impossible questions. And to waste your life searching for answers you can't find would be as big a loss as the war."

He mumbled, "Guess so."

"I expect your dad would want to know he had made it possible for you to have a happy life. You wouldn't want to disappoint him, would you?"

Robbie shook his head.

"I can tell you still aren't convinced."

The boy nodded. "I know what you're trying to say, but sometimes it's too hard."

"I know. I don't know how I'd cope if I couldn't have my music. And if I couldn't pray about things. Do you have anything that makes you feel better?"

Robbie's eyes brightened. "The horses. I like being with the horses. Every night I brush them and talk to them."

"That's something good, isn't it?"

He nodded. "And I like your music. It makes me feel good inside."

She squeezed his arm. "Thank you, Robbie. That's the nicest thing anyone's said to me in a long time."

The boy ducked his head, but not before she caught the pleased smile.

"I'll play something for you now if you like."

"Could you come home with me and play for Dad? He liked it so much the other day."

"I'd like that very much."

They fell into step.

"I like your family a lot," she said.

"Me, too."

Together they laughed.

"Bet you miss your family."

"I do." She told him about her sisters, the games they played, and the concerts they gave. "We had a grand time."

"Violet and Junior are too little to play games."

She studied the small, serious boy at her side. The load he carried was great for so young a child, but she sensed he needed only some guidance and reassurance to shoulder it. "I'm the oldest, too," she said. "My sisters would be about the same age span as Violet and Frankie Junior are to you. I had to be patient with my younger sisters as they learned to do things, but it was always a great deal of fun." She considered her words carefully. "I know you're a caring boy. In many ways it's up to you whether the younger ones learn to work and play with you."

He cocked his head, searching her face as if hoping to find the answers for the questions and doubts plaguing him. "How's that?"

"As I said, you can teach them not only how to do things but, more important, to want to do them by modelling a positive attitude. You know yourself it's more fun to work with someone who makes the work fun than someone who pushes at you and complains."

The boy walked beside her without speaking, mulling over her words. As they reached the house, he turned to her. "I will always try to be the kind of person they will like to do things with." He stuck out his hand, and she gave it a solemn shake.

"Good for you."

He opened the door and hollered, "Ma, Mrs. Hughes is here!"

Lizzie grabbed his shoulder. "I'd like it if you called me Lizzie. Mrs. Hughes makes me sound like my mother-in-law."

Robbie flashed a cheeky grin. "Ma, Lizzie's here. She said

she'd play the flute for Dad." He ducked back out, calling over his shoulder, "I got to clean out some stalls."

"Come in—come in. I'm right glad to see you again. I hoped you would feel comfortable coming back." Pearl shepherded her inside the kitchen. "You missed Caleb, though. He left awhile ago."

"Then I'll see him at home." But she was disappointed to have missed him. He seemed more relaxed in this home than in his own.

"I'll be making some tea," Pearl said, pushing aside a heap of clothes smelling as if she'd just brought them from the line. "I'm right glad to see you again. My Frankie will be pleased to have you come. He says your music warms his insides." She bustled about boiling water and warming the pot. "Mostly he's cold no matter how much fire I put in the stove. I'm a-thinking it's part his body failing to do its job and part remembrance of the fearsome cold of those trenches. Only God's mercy saw our men through those dreadful days."

"Pearl." A thin voice came from the other room. "Bring her in here to see me."

"We'll be along soon as I pour the tea." Pearl turned back to Lizzie. "Now here I am a-rattling on about me when you're sitting in a strange country, no family of your own, and a man you barely know."

Lizzie blinked at the directness of the woman. "I'm doing all right."

Pearl waved aside her protest as if shooing a fly. "I just want to say, Girl, that I'm here whenever you feel the need of a friend. I'm not to be talking bad about others, but some people'd be a-willing to listen to your hurts and give a stitch or two of encouragement to help mend them hurts, if you know what I'm meaning, while there be others that somehow manage to make the tear larger no matter how innocent their words be." She set a steaming cup in front of Lizzie. "All I'm saying, Lizzie, Girl, is if you find yourself needing some good old-fashioned comfort, you come see Pearl here, and I'll be giving you a hug and a prayer." She turned to the little girl who slipped in the room. "Violet, you take your dad a cup of tea. Now I know I've gone the long road around in my way of saying it, but you understand what I'm meaning, don't you?"

Lizzie nodded. "Thank you." The woman's kind words made it easier to deal with comments such as the postmistress had offered—and her mother-in-law's disapproval.

"Now let's be visiting Frankie." She led the way to her husband's bedside.

"Hello, my dear." Frankie held out a thin hand. "I'm to be doubly blessed with visits from the Hugheses today."

Lizzie met his steady blue eyes without letting her knowledge of his failing health make her falter. "How are you, Frankie?"

"I'm glad to be alive another day. Caleb hurried away, saying he had things to do. What's that man of yours up to?" He lay back against his pillow, taking the cup Violet offered him. "Thank you, Sweetie."

Violet pressed close to her father's side, her eyes adoring him.

Lizzie settled back in her chair. "Seems he's discovered a whole lot of things needing repair around the place. He seems to delight in it. Yesterday, despite his parents' objections, he patched the roof of our house. This morning he fixed the barn roof."

"Good for him." Frankie coughed once, then pressed his lips together and took a slow breath. "Fixing and building are good for him. I expect it helps him forget about the war." He sipped his tea slowly. "Did you happen to bring your flute again?"

"I did." But when she reached for the case, he held up his hand.

"Finish your tea first and tell me how you're liking the new country."

"I like it fine. The spaces, the fresh air, but I think I like the quiet best."

He nodded. "Me, too. No more *rat-a-tat-tat*. Or *ke-boom*." He reached for Pearl's hand. "Home is a mighty nice place."

Pearl leaned over and kissed his forehead. " 'Tis mighty nice to have you here."

Lizzie set aside her now-empty cup and picked up her flute. "Is there anything special you'd like to hear?"

"Anything at all, but I really liked that last one you played the other day."

She played several songs as Pearl and Frankie held hands with Violet, who was cuddled between them. Junior slipped in and leaned against his mother's shoulder. For a moment after she finished, no one spoke. Then Pearl shook herself.

"Makes me feel good right here." She touched her chest.

Lizzie put the flute away. "I must go. Caleb will be wondering where I've gone."

The Duncans made her promise she'd come again soon.

But when she returned home, Caleb seemed not to have noticed her absence. He was atop the barn again, painting the last of the new shingles. He paused only long enough to wave.

A short while later, she heard more hammering and looked out to see him repairing the trim around the windows in the barn.

When he came in for tea, he brought his bucket of nails and the hammer. "I thought I'd check the cupboards to see if they needed fixing," he said after he'd eaten. He opened each door and tightened the hinges. He pounded in several nails to reinforce the shelves beside the stove, then made a tour of the room, checking the window frames and pounding nails into the doorsills to tighten them.

The next morning, the sound of hammering accompanied Lizzie as she washed the grime from all the windows. Caleb had begun repairs on the corral fences.

That night he climbed into bed beside her and sighed. "Funny how I never noticed before how many nails are missing around this place."

She cuddled close, but he seemed not to notice as he rushed on to describe the task ahead of him. "I had a look around the barn, and there isn't a stall or gate that isn't in need of a few nails here or there."

She eased back. "I washed the windows today."

"After I finish fixing up the barn, I'm going to check the fences."

Lizzie crossed her hands over her stomach, wishing he would show as much enthusiasm for her as he did his bucket of nails; then remembering Frankie's words, she scolded herself. It was good for Caleb to be able to fix things. And at least he was here at her side, not slouched in the chair in the other room. She snuggled against him, pressing her face to his shoulder until she fell asleep.

❧

She jerked awake, her heart beating hard enough to make her gasp for breath. Her senses instantly alert, she strained to identify whatever had awakened her, at first seeing, hearing nothing. Then Caleb yelled out in his sleep, and she jumped so hard her neck hurt.

"Caleb? What's the matter?" She shook his arm.

He yelled again, sounds garbled and unintelligible, yet tortured enough to send shivers across her shoulders.

"Caleb." She shook him harder. "Wake up. Wake up."

"Umph." His breath exploded. He groaned and flung the covers off to sit on the edge of the bed. The trees streaked the moonlight coming through the window like long fingers scraping at the room. In the metal gray light, Lizzie saw Caleb huddled at the side of the bed, his head in his hands.

She scooted to his side and, draping her feet over the side of the bed, wrapped her arm around him. "It was a dream, Caleb. Only a dream."

A shudder shook him like a rag caught in the wind.

She held him tighter. "It's all right now. You're here with me. Safe and sound."

He shivered again.

She wrapped both arms around his chest. For a moment he was stiff and resistant; then he groaned and buried his face against her hair.

"I dreamt I was back in France. The artillery shells were getting closer and closer, but I was knee-deep in mud and couldn't move." His voice echoed with fear and pain. "I saw August and Gustave, but I couldn't move or call out to warn them. I couldn't pull them back to safety. My feet were stuck. August twisted as a bullet hit him. Then Gustave fell." He choked back a sob. "I couldn't do anything but stand there and watch them die." He flung away from her. "They all died." He rocked back and forth.

Lizzie felt him turning inward, away from her.

"I wish I had died."

"No!" The word ripped from her. "Thank God you came back safe and sound." Though she wondered how sound. "He spared you for a reason."

"Six of us went. Me and Frankie, Gustave and August Carlson. Dick and George Leeds. They all died but me and

Frankie, and poor Frankie is more dead than alive." He jerked to his feet. She could feel him standing over her, feel the heat of his anger and frustration. In the shifting gray shadows, she saw his fist clenched inches from her face. "Why didn't I die, too? Why should I be spared?" He yelled the words.

She shrank back, her insides quaking at this angry, loud stranger before her. "I don't know why. I only know you have your whole life ahead of you." Taking a deep breath, she wrapped her hands around his fist.

He jerked from her as if she'd burnt him. "I have nothing. I am nothing."

"You have me." The words wrenched from her. She wanted to be enough for him—enough to heal his pain. She wanted him to turn to her and hold her and say, "Yes, of course. How could I forget?"

But he stumbled into his pants and stomped into his boots. Not bothering with his shirt, he staggered from the room, muttering, "I've had enough. Enough."

She dashed after him, but he had already thrown open the door and disappeared into the darkness. She stood in the open doorway, hearing him mutter as he rushed headlong into the night. With a strangled cry, she raced back to the bedroom and pulled on a robe and shoved her feet into her shoes, but when she returned to the door, she could no longer hear him. She strained for several minutes, but with no idea of what direction he had taken, she stood in the door, shivering, uncertain what she should do.

A coyote howled in the distance. A cow near the barn mooed, a low mournful sound that made Lizzie hug her arms around her.

She rubbed her arms as the chill of the night stole through her body.

six

The silence deepened, broken only by regular night sounds. Lizzie shook so violently, she had to lean against the door frame. Finally, chilled and defeated, she closed the door and hurried back to bed to huddle under the covers, shivering. She stared at the clawing shadows on the wall as her thoughts turned inside out.

"Enough," he'd said.

What did he mean? Her fears swelled, crowding her lungs until she could barely squeeze in a breath. Would he do something foolish?

"Please, God. Please, God." She muttered the words over and over, her fists clenched, her eyes stinging. *Don't take him from me. Fix his agony.*

The gray light took on a ghostly yellow pallor as the sun worked toward the horizon. Somewhere a bird rattled his beak against a tree trunk.

Lizzie turned toward the window, listening.

It wasn't a bird. It was Caleb hammering. Her chest rose as she filled her lungs. "Thank You, God," she murmured and fell asleep.

❧

Time passed into a long string of tense days. As the evening light of this particular day faded, Lizzie waited for Caleb to return. Finally, accepting it would be another lonely night like so many others, she prepared for bed. If she'd hoped for an improvement after the nightmare of two weeks ago, her hopes had been cruelly dashed. Caleb had sunk into a sea of despondency. Often he rushed from the house as darkness descended. She'd watched him pace up and down the road enough times to know he was fleeing demons in his mind.

How she ached to be able to help him, but he jerked away if she mentioned anything about his nightmares or his memories from the war. She longed for someone to confide in. Once she'd broached the subject with Mother Hughes.

"Caleb worries me some days," she'd begun, hoping Mother Hughes would offer a word of wisdom or comfort.

"You really didn't get to know him well, did you?" Her words were gently spoken; yet Lizzie felt barbs tear at her. Before she could protest, Mother Hughes went on in her soft voice. "Caleb always was independently minded." The smile on her mother-in-law's face did not disguise her displeasure. "Like fixing the roof on the Sabbath," Mother Hughes continued. "He simply had to prove he could make his own rules."

Lizzie had kept her face turned downward, watching the swirling darkness of her tea. Mother Hughes didn't come right out and say it, but she gave Lizzie the impression Caleb was getting what he deserved for ignoring some of their wishes. How could her mother-in-law be so wrong in her judgment of Caleb? And so unfeeling? Caleb tried his best to please them, going against their wishes only when he felt he had to. "He has to answer to his own conscience." It was on the tip of her tongue to add that he had to face his own turmoil as well, but her mother-in-law sighed, a sound filled with sad resignation.

"Unfortunately we can't make our own rules. We have to live by the ones God has set."

"Of course." Lizzie said no more, knowing their views were so widely separated they couldn't agree on Caleb's motivation.

Lizzie crawled into the cold, lonely bed and stared into the darkness. Tomorrow she would write home again. She'd been postponing it for fear she would give away her distress and cause worry for those at home, but if she didn't write soon, they would worry anyway.

And maybe she'd talk to Pearl. She'd been to visit several times, always cheered by the homey, loving atmosphere, but she was reluctant to add her concerns to the load Pearl already carried, even though she knew Pearl wouldn't see it that way. Suddenly she ached to share the load and be assured everything would be fine.

Toward morning, Caleb stomped into the house and fell on the bed, fully clothed. Lizzie waited until he snored softly before she pulled a blanket over him. In sleep, his face was young and untroubled, a marked contrast to the deep shadowed worry it carried during the day.

"Caleb, my love." She stroked his cheek, a gesture he would have pulled away from if he were awake. "What horrors fill your poor mind?" She sat on the edge of the bed and watched him sleep, finally admitting her fears. What if he was lost forever to her? A moan ripped through her. She stifled it for fear of waking Caleb.

After awhile, she lay down beside him. Although she knew she wouldn't sleep again, she coveted this time of peacefulness at his side.

When he came from the bedroom a few hours later, she stood at the stove stirring porridge.

"Good morning." She smiled at the sleep lines on his cheek. "How are you?"

He stretched. "Ready for another day." He squinted at her. "How about you? Seems like days since I've talked to you."

A warm glow ignited somewhere behind her heart at his acknowledgment. "You've been busy."

He nodded. "Seems no end of things to fix."

"Are you all finished then?" Perhaps she'd misjudged the situation, and it was only the press of work that had driven him these last few days. "Breakfast is ready."

He perched on the edge of his chair, pausing to mutter a grace before he gulped down his food. "I've got to fix the fence." His brow furrowed as he pushed from the table; grabbed his pail containing nails, pliers, hammer, and an assortment of screws, fencing staples, and other items; and rushed from the house.

Lizzie fell back, admitting this compulsion was not eagerness for work.

Immediately after she'd cleaned up the breakfast things, she kneaded bread dough, according to instructions from Pearl, and set it to rise. Unable to put her mind to any other task, she pulled out her writing materials. But words would not come. At least not words to send back home. Instead she took a plain piece of paper and sketched a picture of Robbie as she remembered him sitting on the rock, watching her play the flute. The picture made her smile. Robbie, despite the worries he carried about his father, always wore an impish grin she hadn't noticed until she sketched his likeness. If Robbie could face life with humor and goodwill, could she do any less, despite her worries over Caleb?

Smiling now, she drew another picture showing her standing under the tree playing her flute for Robbie. She filled the bare branches with budding leaves, then stared at what she had drawn. She dashed to the window to study the trees. Spring had indeed arrived while she fretted about other things. Spring, a time of renewal and refreshment. She hummed as she began a letter to her family.

A knock interrupted her.

"Come in," she called. Mother Hughes entered, carrying her offering of eggs.

Lizzie glanced at the clock. Mother Hughes didn't normally come until after lunch, but it was barely eleven o'clock. "You're early today." Lizzie slid the kettle to the hottest part of the stove.

"I won't stop for tea today," the older woman said. "I have a busy day planned." Her gaze rested on the pages on the table.

Lizzie refrained the urge to scoop them out of her sight.

"I'm going to wash windows." Mother Hughes's tone and glance around the house suggested Lizzie should occupy herself with something more productive than drawing pictures.

Lizzie smiled. Her windows sparkled. Her house was tidy and clean. The bread dough punched up round as a fat tummy under the tea towel.

Mother Hughes smiled. "I guess you don't have as much to do as I. Spring work is upon us. There'll be gardening. And Father is struggling, trying to do it all himself."

Lizzie felt the sting of criticism directed at Caleb. With no notion of what spring work entailed, she didn't know what Mother Hughes expected from her son.

The older woman retreated outdoors. "I'll leave you to your amusements."

Lizzie stared at the closed door. Somehow Mother Hughes had a way of making even the most innocent of remarks sound like censor. Shrugging, she finished her letter before she turned her attention to making the noon meal.

"Your mother brought the eggs early today," she said later as she served the meal.

Caleb's fork halted halfway to his mouth, and he lifted startled eyes to her. "Oh," he muttered.

"Yes, she said there was a lot of work to do. Time for spring work, she said."

He nodded. "Yeah."

"What does she mean by 'spring work'?" She guessed it didn't mean simply washing the windows.

"Ploughing, planting. Stuff like that."

He seemed detached about it.

"I see," she said. "It's a lot of work, I assume."

He gulped the last of his food and pushed back from the table. "I've got to finish the fence." He rushed outside.

The house seemed to close in on her after he left. She grabbed her flute case and her letter and headed for the Duncan home.

Violet sat on the step, playing with a rag doll, as Lizzie turned in at the gate. "Where's your mother?" Lizzie asked.

The child turned her steady gaze upon Lizzie. "In'na garden." She eyed the flute case. "You gonna play for us?"

Lizzie sat beside the girl. "Would you like that?" Over the past days the younger children had lost their shyness with her.

Violet nodded, a smile creasing her face. "You want to see my daddy?"

Lizzie hugged her. "I think I'll go see your mother first. May I leave my flute here beside you?"

Violet nodded.

Lizzie went around the house to where Pearl and Robbie worked with shovels, turning over the garden soil.

Pearl pressed her hand into the small of her back and stretched when she saw Lizzie. "I am right glad to see you. Gives me an excuse for a break."

"Don't let me keep you from your work," Lizzie protested.

"You're doing me a favor." Pearl handed her shovel to Robbie. "Put these away for now."

After Robbie left, Pearl turned to study Lizzie's face with an intensity that made Lizzie blink.

"Now don't you go minding my nosiness," Pearl said. "But I'm wanting to know you're not holding on to troubles that would be best shared with a friend." When Lizzie didn't answer, unsure what to say, Pearl continued. "I see that man of yours every day, and I see darkness behind his eyes. There's something deep and hard troubling that man."

Lizzie nodded. "It frightens me."

Pearl grabbed her hand. "You telling me you're afraid of Caleb?"

Lizzie hadn't thought of it that way. "I don't think so, though sometimes he gets very angry. No. I'm not afraid for me. I'm afraid for him. Maybe—" The words were too terrible to say.

Pearl nodded. "You think maybe he's gone too far into his nightmares to come back?"

Lizzie hung her head. "It isn't as if he's gone out of his head or anything. Maybe I'm making a mountain out of a molehill."

"You know what you see even if you pretend to yourself you don't." She squeezed Lizzie's hands, and Lizzie clung to her with a desperation that made her cheeks grow warm. But she couldn't help herself. Pearl had put Lizzie's fears right out in the open where she could no longer pretend they didn't exist. "Girl, I know what it's like. I faced my own fears and fought my battle with self-pity and resentment. And you know what I found?" Lizzie shook her head. "It's all a grand waste of time. Best to take what life hands you and make the best of it." Her eyes narrowed as she studied Lizzie. "Unless you got a mind to walk away from it all."

Lizzie shook her head. "I love Caleb. For better or worse."

"Good. My sentiments exactly. Besides, I'm that grateful to

have my Frankie for however long the good Lord sees fit to leave him. I want the children to get to know him again. I want them to have good memories of him."

"Does Frankie—?" She broke off, embarrassed at what she'd been about to ask.

"Does he what?" Pearl's voice was gentle, inviting her to ask what she wanted.

"Does he have nightmares?"

"My, yes. He says he has only to close his eyes to see it all again. Like it was branded to the inside of his head. He cries out. Sudden loud noises set his nerves twitching."

Lizzie nodded. "The nightmares are the worst." She studied Pearl, wondering if she dared ask the rest.

"Something else is troubling you, Child. What is it?"

"Does Frankie let you touch him? Seems Caleb doesn't even know me sometimes."

Pearl's face crinkled into kindly lines. "Poor Caleb. Poor Lizzie. I'm thinking Caleb suffers more than Frankie."

"How can that be? Frankie—his feet, his lungs." She shook her head.

"Don't you see? Poor Caleb came back whole and well. The only one. Can you imagine the load of guilt that poor man carries?"

Lizzie pressed her lips together, her insides quaking with pain for Caleb's suffering. "But what can I do?" she whispered.

"Girl, I wish I had the answers. Not only for you but for myself. All I can tell you, Lizzie, Girl, is love your man and pray to God for a miracle."

Lizzie nodded.

"Now come along. Frankie will have heard your voice. He'll accuse me of keeping you for myself." Pearl laughed. "He does like your music."

"Has Caleb been today?"

"Not yet, but he's not one to often miss a day."

She followed Pearl indoors, Violet at her side, carrying the flute proudly. Junior sprawled on the floor beside his father's bed, coloring a picture. He grinned at Lizzie as she entered.

"I've been waiting for you to decide to visit me," Frankie said. "I thought Pearl was going to hog you to herself."

Pearl rolled her eyes. "What did I tell you?"

Lizzie laughed. "Exactly that."

Frankie gave his wife an adoring look. "She reads me like a page, doesn't she?" He grabbed Pearl's hand and pulled her to him. "And I love it." He lifted his face and kissed her.

Pearl's cheeks turned pink. "Go away with you. What will Lizzie think?"

"Probably that you're a very lucky woman to have the likes of me begging for a kiss." For a moment his expression turned bleak; then he brightened. "I see you brought your flute."

"Would I dare come without it?" She grinned at them all.

"I hope not," Frankie said.

"What will it be first? Talk or music?"

"Sit and talk," Frankie said. "Tell me what that man of yours is up to. Seems he's always in a rush to finish some job or other. Barely sits down long enough to visit."

Lizzie and Pearl exchanged looks.

Frankie's eyes narrowed. "What are you two not saying?"

Pearl nodded at Lizzie. "You tell him while Violet and Junior help me make tea. Come along, you two."

Junior scrambled after his mother, but Violet hesitated.

"We'll come back for the music." Pearl shepherded them out of the room.

Frankie watched her with sharp interest. "Is something wrong with Caleb?"

"Not in the way you're thinking." She shrugged. "It's hard to put into words but he—well, he seems driven by something inside him."

"I guessed that."

"He can hardly sleep. He wanders around half the night and falls into bed just before dawn. And he won't stop fixing things."

Frankie chuckled. "I don't mean to laugh, but somehow I can picture Caleb with a hammer and screwdriver ferreting out every loose nail and screw on the farm."

"It's worse than that. Now he's taken to nailing slats on the barbwire fence around the farm."

Frankie shrugged. "Maybe pounding nails will drive the torment from him." He stared at the ceiling. "We saw a lot of horrible things." He closed his eyes. "Things too horrible even to talk about."

She nodded. That much she understood; but now that it was over, why couldn't he put it behind him? Why wasn't she enough to make him forget? Why wasn't her love enough?

Frankie continued. "Nighttime is the worst. You can't get away from your thoughts." He turned wide, desperate eyes on her. "Give him time. Let him work it out. He'll get better. I know he will."

She blinked back tears, pressing her lips together. The agony in Frankie's voice did nothing to encourage her.

☙

The next day, Lizzie found a shovel, dug a border around the house, and planted flower seeds she'd brought from the garden at home. On her hands and knees, pressing seeds into place, she didn't hear Mother Hughes's approach.

"So you've decided to plant a garden."

Lizzie sat back on her heels. "I brought seeds from the flowers at home."

"Flowers? You'd be better to spend your time growing something useful."

Lizzie refused to let her mother-in-law's words ruffle her. "I plan on having a vegetable garden, too, but flowers will make the place look nice." She brushed off her skirt as she stood. "Don't you like flowers?"

Mother Hughes sniffed. "I've never had time for such nonsense."

Lizzie took the basket of eggs the older woman held toward her. "Why, isn't that a shame?"

"Whatever do you mean?"

"Only that God has filled the earth with beauty and goodness. We should allow ourselves time to enjoy it."

"Humph." Mother Hughes turned away. "Some of us can ill afford the luxury. God has given us work to occupy ourselves with."

Lizzie held her tongue as her mother-in-law marched away.

She pressed the last of the seeds into place, then walked to the side of the house to the spot she had chosen for the vegetable garden. She stuck the shovel into the ground and lifted the sod. It was far harder than she'd imagined. How would she plant a garden here? Perhaps Caleb had a better idea. She went in search of him. He wasn't hard to find. She simply followed the sound of pounding until she found him down the road nailing slats to the barbwire fence. The slatted fence marched along the boundary past the barn and turned the corner. If he kept it up, the farm would be surrounded like a fortress.

She called out to him.

He straightened, his hammer poised to drive in another nail. He had unbuttoned his shirt and slipped his arms out so the garment hung from his belt like a flag.

"I'd like to put in a vegetable garden, but there's only sod by the house. Is there someplace else?" She stood close enough to see the sheen of sweat on his skin and to observe how rail thin he was. She could smell the salty scent of his sweat. How she longed to hold him and comfort him as one comforts a child. If only he would let her. Surely it would heal his nightmares. She reached out a hand and pressed it to his chest.

He quivered but did not draw back.

"I've missed you," she whispered.

"I'm right here." His voice thickened.

"That's the trouble," she murmured. "You're here." She nodded toward the fence. "I want you here." She pressed her other hand to her chest.

He dropped the hammer and stepped closer, trapping her hands between them. "Like this?"

She lifted her face and met his eyes steadily. "This is a good start."

He searched her eyes as if looking for something illusive. She held his gaze, letting him see deep into her heart, praying he would find his answer and satisfy his need.

He grasped her chin and slowly lowered his head.

She stretched to meet his kiss.

He crushed her to his chest, his kiss deepening until she floated in a swell of emotion. He broke away, pressed her head to his shoulder, and moaned. "I don't deserve you."

She laughed, although she felt him pulling back into himself. "You're stuck with me whether or not you deserve it."

"Come on." He took her hand. "Let's get out of here."

She followed willingly. He took her to the house. "Wait here. I have to get something." He ducked inside, returning with a large, bulky package. "Something for Frankie," he said.

Hand in hand, they walked toward the Duncan home.

seven

In Frankie's bedroom, Caleb handed over the parcel.

"What is it?" Frankie asked.

"Open it and see. It's something you've wanted a long time."

Frankie studied him a moment longer.

"Open it, Daddy," Junior begged, bouncing on the balls of his feet.

"Hurry, Daddy," Violet said. Turning toward Lizzie, she added, "Caleb brings Daddy good presents."

"Really? Tell me about them."

She pointed toward a seascape that looked as if it had been cut from a magazine and framed. Lizzie recognized the frame as being similar to the ones Caleb had made for her. "He gave Daddy that picture. Daddy says it makes him feel good looking at it."

Frankie ruffled Violet's hair. "That it does, Sweetie." He lifted his gaze to Lizzie. "I feel like I'm free as that bird hovering over the water." His gaze shifted to Caleb. "No more stuck in one place."

"No more stuck," Caleb echoed.

Junior touched the scarf Frankie always wore around his neck. "Caleb gave him this."

"No more freezing," Frankie muttered, his gaze never flickering from Caleb.

"Open the present," Violet demanded.

Pearl pulled the two children back to lean on her knee. "You best give your daddy some room."

Frankie lowered his gaze slowly. He broke the string and tore back the brown paper to reveal a pair of sturdy, black leather boots with thick soles. He ran his hands along the smooth leather and cleared his throat.

Caleb cleared his throat as well.

Lizzie glanced back and forth between the men, noting how they avoided looking at anyone. The room echoed with silence. She watched with wonder the emotions play across Frankie's face—pain, sadness, then hope and resignation.

"Thank you, Caleb." Frankie finally managed, his voice sounding tight. "But I think you can use these more than I can."

"I want you to know you'll never have cold, wet feet again," said Caleb.

"Thank you," Frankie murmured again. "Put them on the shelf next to Petey, will you, Pearl?"

Pearl set the children aside and placed the boots beside the mouse cage. They all stood in a circle, silently admiring the boots.

"Well, now." Pearl clapped her hands. "The good doctor will be along shortly to see about Daddy, and I need you children out of the way. So you run along outside. Robbie is in the barn. Go find him and tell him to watch out for you."

The two youngsters scampered to do as they were told.

One look at Frankie's face, and Lizzie knew the doctor's visit was not anticipated. "Is there anything I can do?" she asked Pearl.

Pearl and Frankie exchanged glances. Some unspoken message passed between them. Her expression tight, Pearl turned back to Lizzie. "If it's not asking too much, it would ease both our minds if you could take the children to your place until the doctor's done." She swallowed hard, struggling visibly to keep back tears. "The doctor has to clean Frankie's feet." She bit her bottom lip before she continued. "You see, it's quite painful," she whispered.

"It's no problem at all, is it, Caleb?" Caleb turned away, but not before she saw the dark, hollow look on his face. Her heart dropped. Whatever goodness their visit to this home had accomplished fled as quickly as it came. "I'll gather them up and take them home for tea. Are you coming, Caleb?"

He muttered something unintelligible and strode from the room. She wondered if he would walk away without her, but he waited at the edge of the yard as she collected the children.

The two younger ones raced ahead, eagerly exploring every rock and fallen branch.

Robbie walked beside Caleb and her, as lost in thought as the adults.

"Were you working in the barn?" Lizzie asked, determined to lift the mood.

"Yeah. I was brushing the team."

Caleb lifted his head. "Why is there a team at home?"

"Audie couldn't get anyone to drive the wagon. Mom says we lost a job because of it."

"You should have called me. I could take a load."

Robbie nodded. "I'll tell Mom." After a moment, he added, "Audie says he's tired of running the business. Says he only figured on helping out Dad until the war was over. Now, he says, the war is over, but Dad ain't ever going to take over again." Robbie's shoulders drooped.

"What does your mother say?" Caleb demanded.

"I never told her," Robbie mumbled. "She tries her best."

"Good lad. Let's keep it to ourselves for the time being."

"It's all right by me."

As they approached the house, the younger children ground

to a halt, and Violet turned to face Lizzie. "What will we do?"

Lizzie grinned. "I know lots to do."

Caleb groaned. "She'll have you playing all sorts of games and playacting."

"Really?" Violet looked intrigued.

"What would you prefer?" Lizzie asked. "A game of tag or a game of pretend?"

"Tag!" Junior shouted.

"Pretend!" Violet said.

Lizzie laughed and touched Robbie's shoulder. "You're it." She darted away.

The others scattered. For a moment Caleb looked as if he might like to join them, but then he muttered, "I've got to finish the fence."

The children screamed and giggled as they chased back and forth. Lizzie laughed as she hadn't in a long time. Not since she'd left England.

Finally, sweating and breathless, they collapsed in a heap.

"Can we play pretend now?" Violet asked.

"As soon as I catch my breath."

Robbie stirred himself. "I'm going to help Caleb."

Lizzie watched him go, then turned to the others. "What would you like to pretend?" They gave her blank looks. "I know. Let's pretend we're sailing a ship across the ocean in that picture your daddy has." She looked around until she found a nice tall stick and stuck it into the ground next to a tree. "Here's our mast. You, Junior, find something to make a hat out of, and you can be the captain. Violet and I will climb the rigging and see if any other boats are on the sea with us."

Violet scrambled up one tree and Lizzie up another while Junior picked up a stick for a sword and marched back and forth saying, "I'm a cap'in."

Later, Caleb and Robbie came to the house to share sand-wiches, milk, and cookies. The children helped clean up.

"I guess it's time to take the children home." She met Caleb's eyes, hoping he would offer to accompany them.

He nodded. "Let's go."

The five of them marched back toward town, quieter now, but with a peaceful contentment. When Lizzie took Caleb's hand, he pulled her close. A sense of rightness filled her. Surely Caleb would be okay now.

Pearl sat on the steps of the house plucking at the hem of her skirt. The five of them stopped in front of her. "Did you have a good time?" she asked.

Lizzie caught the sound of tears in her voice and whispered to Caleb, "Take the children inside."

Robbie hesitated, but after Caleb whispered something in his ear, he followed the others.

Lizzie sat beside the other woman and wrapped her arms around her shoulders. Something she'd heard someplace came to her mind: It's the women who bear the pain of war most quietly.

Pearl leaned into her embrace, a sob shaking her.

"You go right ahead and cry," Lizzie said. "You've had to be strong for everyone else far too long."

Pearl cried softly a few minutes, then sniffed and sat up, scrubbing her eyes with her hands. "It was awful. Frankie tried to be brave, but it hurt so much he screamed." Pearl shuddered. "I could see for myself his feet are worse."

Lizzie didn't say anything. What could she say in the face of such suffering?

Pearl sighed. "I must go to the children. They'll be worrying."

"Frankie?" Lizzie half feared what she'd find inside.

"The doctor gave him something to ease the pain." She

pushed herself to her feet. "It did little to help whilst the doctor was working, but at least it made him able to sleep now it's over." She shuddered. "I'm hoping he sleeps the night."

Indoors, Caleb had the children clustered around the table. Pearl thanked him, then addressed the children. "Daddy's sleeping so I want you to be as quiet as possible."

They nodded. The two younger ones hopped down and went to their bedroom, but Robbie stayed at the table, his eyes never leaving his mother's face.

"Is Dad all right?"

Pearl faced him squarely. "He's plumb wore out after the doctor's visit. He'll be right as can be after he's rested."

Robbie's expression hardened. Lizzie wondered if he believed his father would ever be "right as can be" again.

Caleb had been standing to one side, watching the exchange, his arms crossed over his chest. Now he grunted and dropped his arms, his fists clenched at his side. "Give my regards to Frankie," he muttered, heading for the door.

Lizzie sprang after him. "Caleb, wait."

He glanced over his shoulder, as if startled to remember she was there.

"My thanks for your help," Pearl called after them.

Lizzie practically ran to keep up with Caleb. "Slow down," she begged, but he acted as if he didn't hear. "Caleb." She tried again. "I'm getting winded." She grabbed his arm.

He jumped as if she'd struck him.

"Caleb. It's only me." She clung to his arm, forcing him to slow down.

He faced her, his fists raised defensively in front of him, a wild expression in his eyes as he rocked on the balls of his feet.

Lizzie jerked back, her mouth suddenly parched, her heart

drumming in her ears. "Caleb?" Her voice squeaked. "Don't hit me."

Caleb stood poised and tense, blinked once, and slowly lowered his fists. "Sorry," he mumbled, shoving his hands in his pockets. "Thought I heard something."

She exhaled loudly, her heart still racing. "You frightened me."

"Sorry," he mumbled again.

Lizzie blinked. Sorry wasn't good enough. It was time to confront Caleb's problems. "There must be something I can do to help you."

He kicked at the ground. "Can you erase my mind?"

"Of course not." The idea made her shudder. "I wouldn't want to. What would become of the good things in it?"

"The same thing that would happen to the bad things. They'd be gone." The harshness in his voice grated along her nerves.

"Caleb. I don't want to lose you."

He marched on without turning. She hastened to keep up, to catch what he said. "Maybe you already have."

Her blood turned cold at the finality of his words. "No." The cry wrenched from her. "No. I won't believe that."

He snorted, a sound filled with helpless despair.

Lizzie followed him home in the dusk of the evening, praying for a way to get through to him, for words to break through his despair. Somehow she must prove to him it wasn't too late. She practiced a speech, changing it several times, but at the door he turned aside.

"Things to do," he mumbled and strode away.

Lizzie pressed her palms to her chest, holding back the ache in her heart. Hot tears trailed down her cheeks. She longed to run after him but knew he wouldn't hear anything she had to say. Her limbs heavy, she went inside to a gloomy, lonely room, praying silently for understanding. For patience. For a miracle. She wanted to trust God. She knew He could help. But it was hard being shut out time after time.

Sometime in the almost-daylight hours of early morning, Caleb stumbled in and threw himself on top of the bed. He said not a word nor made any attempt to touch her.

Lizzie turned on her side, a toothache-like pain eating at her insides.

&

Lizzie stabbed the shovel into the ground, searching for a spot that would yield to her efforts.

"Are you looking for something in particular?" It was Father Hughes.

"Yes. A place where I can dig a garden spot."

He took off his hat and scratched his head. "Nothing but virgin sod around here. Best thing you could do is lift the sod and set it aside. Use the soil underneath."

"I see. Thank you." Father Hughes continued toward the barn.

Several hours later, dripping with sweat, Lizzie measured her progress and decided she would have a very small garden plot. Just then Caleb marched into sight across the yard. Lizzie called him. "Can I get you to help for a few minutes?" She wasn't sure if he'd agree. In the two days since their walk home from the Duncans', he'd avoided her as much as humanly possible.

"What do you need?"

She indicated the bare soil and the pile of sods. "I'm trying to prepare a garden spot. I could sure use some help with the digging."

He grabbed the shovel and stabbed it into the ground, turning over a clump of musky-smelling earth. He moved back, stabbing again and again, turning over a row of clumps.

Lizzie watched the rich earth yielding to his attack. He worked with sharp, quick jabs, grunting as the shovel encountered resistance. His frenzied movements didn't seem quite right. His face muscles twitched. His eyes had a dead, hollow look. His grunts grew louder, more agony than effort.

A shiver snaked across her shoulders. She wrapped her arms around herself, squishing the material of her sleeves. "Caleb?"

He didn't respond.

She spoke his name louder.

He threw the shovel down so hard it bounced twice, and he gasped. "I hate digging in the dirt." He jerked away and strode off. A few minutes later, she heard the sound of hammering along the fence line.

She rubbed her chest, trying to ease the tightness that made each breath painful. When she could move without feeling brittle, she picked up the shovel, carried it to the house, and leaned it against the wall. Perhaps later, when her arms stopped shaking, she would go back to preparing a garden spot.

After the noon meal, after Caleb had disappeared again, she returned to the garden. The ground was stubborn, resistant to her efforts, but she doggedly turned over clump after clump, ignoring her aching shoulders and the blisters forming on her palms.

"What'cha doing?"

She jumped in alarm and spun around to face Robbie. "You gave me a fright." She expelled her breath in a gust. "I'm trying to make a garden."

"Looks like a lot of work."

"It is." But work made it easy not to think about the changes in Caleb.

"I could help." He took the shovel.

She sat on the pile of sods. "Thanks. Whew! I'm hot."

"I bet you could use some of Mom's garden space."

"I wouldn't want to have to run into town every time I felt like pulling a few weeds."

"Guess not." He worked steadily.

"I'm going to fix us something to drink." She filled a pitcher with cold water from the pump and carried it to the garden, laughing at her optimistic reference to the bare patch of brown soil. "I call this my garden," she told Robbie. "Even though it so stubbornly refuses to be tamed."

Robbie sat beside her and gulped a cup of water. "Nothin's easy, is it?"

"Robbie, you're much too young to be so pessimistic."

"What does that mean?"

"Well, I suppose it means you don't expect good things to happen."

He shrugged. "What good things are there?"

She studied the boy at her side. "Something's troubling you, isn't it?"

He nodded and turned to face her. "Mom tries to pretend everything is okay, but I know my dad's not getting better."

She bit the inside of her lip. Robbie was right. Things weren't easy.

"I'm right, aren't I?"

She thought about her answer. It wasn't her right to tell this child things his mother didn't want him to know. Finally she said, "Your mother is grateful your dad is able to come home. She wants you all to have good memories."

Robbie thought about it awhile. "I don't want my dad to die."

There was nothing she could say. No words of comfort could ease the pain and dread he faced.

"I'm so afraid sometimes."

She nodded, wanting to say, *Me, too—I'm afraid, too.*

"Robbie, I can't promise you it will be easy. I can't pretend you don't have hard things to deal with. But I can pray for you."

"Right now?"

"Certainly." They bowed together. Lizzie folded her hands and prayed, "Father God, You know Your child Robbie has difficult things to deal with. I ask You to give him patience and wisdom and strength. I ask You to ease his father's pain and be with the rest of the family. Thank You for hearing and answering our prayers. Amen."

They sat in quiet reflection as she silently prayed for herself and Caleb.

"What about you?"

She blinked. "What about me?"

"You and Caleb."

She watched him, wondering what this lad saw.

"Before the war, Caleb was different. He was fun and easy."

"That's how I remember him, too."

"Now he acts like he's scared and mad and—I don't know— he's just different."

She nodded, amazed at his perceptiveness. "It's hard to forget the horrible things he saw during the war."

"Will he? Will he ever forget?"

It was a question she had asked herself many times. And didn't like the answer. "I don't suppose he will." She rushed on with the arguments she had given herself time and again. "But perhaps it will fade with time. Maybe he'll learn to put it behind him." She blinked back tears and whispered, "I simply don't know."

He jumped up and started digging again. "Like I said, ain't nothin' easy."

She couldn't argue.

∂

The next day, Father Hughes stopped by the house. "Letter from home," he called.

She rushed out to take the letters, feeling she'd been handed a pocketful of hope.

"Caleb said he'd get the horses hitched up and start ploughing," Father Hughes said, looking pleased at the prospect.

"Yes, he said spring work was waiting." She nodded and rushed inside, settling herself on the rocking chair before she tore open the first letter and eagerly read the news from her sisters. The second envelope contained a letter from Father. She read it once quickly, then again, more slowly, chewing the words in her mind.

> *Dear Elizabeth,*
> *I have read a great deal about the veterans. The news-*
> *papers, especially, are full of horrible stories of men*
> *who have returned, many with dreadful, painful injuries.*
> *Others, it seems from the reports, with no physical*
> *injuries but so affected by the horrors of their experience*
> *that they are profoundly changed, and not for the better.*
> *I've heard accounts of men actually taking their own*
> *lives. I've heard stories of behaviors that made my skin*
> *crawl—stories too awful to repeat. Now you must won-*
> *der why I am telling you this. Or perhaps you already*
> *understand what I am writing of. I know you, my dear*
> *Elizabeth. You are not one to complain or even to tell us*
> *the truth for fear we would worry. But I want you to*
> *know and understand this: If you have found your hus-*
> *band changed beyond recognition, if you are in a situa-*
> *tion where you fear for your safety and sanity, then, dear*
> *child, please do not be afraid to change your mind and*

*come home. Let me know, and I will wire you the money
to return home posthaste.*

*I pray I am speaking of something you are unfamiliar
with, but having said all this, I feel immensely better.*

Your loving father

She closed her eyes and leaned back, a sense of reprieve
easing the tension in her spine she hadn't even been aware of
until this moment. It helped to know she and Caleb were not
the only ones in this situation. And to know her father knew
and had offered her a way of escape, made her breathe easier.
She looked at the letter again. What should she do?

eight

She needed to think about Father's offer, but the house seemed suddenly small and crowded. She folded the letters and shoved them underneath her writing supplies, then hurried outside, pausing to look about her. Although Canada didn't yet feel like home, the wide spaces and fresh, new feel of the land were appealing. England did not pull at her to return.

She turned to study the little house, imagining how the flowers would provide a riot of color against the weathered wood. Despite Caleb's erratic behavior, she had known good times in this little home. She pressed her palms to her stomach.

No, if she stayed or left, it would have nothing to do with the country or the house, and everything to do with Caleb.

Father Hughes had said Caleb had gone plowing. Lizzie struck out toward the field. She rounded the barn and stopped. The horse stood patiently hitched to the plow, but Caleb was nowhere in sight.

Father Hughes came around the other side of the barn and ground to a halt. "Where's Caleb?"

"I thought he was out here."

"Well, he isn't." Father Hughes threw a spanner toward the barn door and stomped toward the plow. "That boy is about as useless as. . ." His muttered words faded as he walked away.

Lizzie stared after him, then looked around the farm, hoping for a glimpse of Caleb. At first she saw nothing; then she thought she saw a flash of dark blue, the color of his shirt, beneath some trees past the barn. Her heart thundering inside her chest, she hurried toward the spot. What was wrong now?

He looked up as she thudded toward to him. "If you've come to tell me I should be plowing, you can forget it."

She shrank back from his accusation. She'd never told him what he should or shouldn't do. "No. I've only come to make sure you're all right."

He bolted to his feet and scowled at her. "Of course I'm all right. Did you think I would try to do myself harm?"

His words were so close to what she'd been thinking that her cheeks burned. "Certainly not." How had the conversation gotten so far out of hand? She'd only come to assure herself there was a shadow of the old Caleb in this angry man before her. She had not come to argue about who said what or what hidden meaning the words contained. But then perhaps she had. In the hidden and shadowed meanings lay the truth about Caleb and her relationship with him.

"Sorry to disappoint you." He stomped away.

She pursed her lips and let her breath out, staring after him as he crossed the pasture, headed away from the farm. In a few minutes, she heard hammering. Building on that annoying fence again. The barricade reached the corner and passed the house and barn in a steady march toward the road.

None of her questions had been answered. In fact, her questions had multiplied.

She followed Caleb's trail, stopping when she could see him bent over the fence. She sat down in the grass, out of sight against a tree, and watched. A mixture of emotions chased around in her head. Which one should she listen to? Her trembling fear at his outburst? Her warm memories of their time in England? And the more recent times of loving in her new home? Was his mind damaged beyond repair? Or did she need to hold on to hope and faith and wait for his healing?

Her legs cramped from huddling over her knees, yet she found no answers. Not from heaven. Not from her heart. And certainly not from Caleb.

She pushed to her feet and ambled back to the house. In the field, Father Hughes plowed a straight furrow. In the big house, she glimpsed Mother Hughes bent over the table. Baking up a storm, no doubt. But Lizzie didn't care. She had something far more important to occupy herself.

It all boiled down to one thing: Did she want to go home? Did she want to give up on Caleb and their marriage? She shook her head. She did not. No matter what problems lay ahead, she wanted to be with Caleb. She would not give up on him. Or them.

Her mind made up, she hurried back to the house, pulled out a piece of paper, and wrote her answer to Father.

> *I will not be coming home, although I cannot pretend*
> *Caleb hasn't changed. He seems haunted by memories of*
> *the war. But I will stay with him. Together we will battle*
> *this demon. I ask only that you keep us in your prayers as*
> *I'm certain you do. I'll write a longer letter later.*
> > *Your loving daughter,*
> > *Elizabeth*

The rattle of a wagon on the road and then a soft "Whoa there" brought Lizzie to her feet. She hurried to the door to see who had stopped outside. "Molly. I'm pleased to see you." They saw each other every Sunday, but Molly's father hurried her away even faster than Lizzie's in-laws hurried her away.

"Pa sent me to town for some things, and I thought, now why don't I take the first road instead of the second and drive past that nice Mrs. Hughes's place and see if she'd like to go to town with me?"

Lizzie laughed. "I'm not used to being Mrs. Hughes. Do you mean me or Caleb's mother?"

Molly wrinkled her nose. "Mrs. Hughes—Caleb's mother—would have a conniption fit if I asked her to ride with me." She ran her hands the length of her body, indicating the man's pants and shirt she wore. "No lady would be caught dead in pants." She so perfectly imitated Mother Hughes's gentle criticism that Lizzie laughed. "So you want to go to town or not?"

"Could you wait while I address an envelope?"

Molly crossed her hands behind her head, leaned back, and put her booted feet up. "I got all the time in the world. If I go home, I'll have to get back to work."

"I'll be but a minute." She scribbled the address on the envelope, waving it to dry the ink before she slipped in the folded pages and sealed it. She went to the side of the wagon. "Do you mind if I run and tell Caleb where I'm going?"

Molly dropped her feet to the wagon floor with a thud. "Where is he?"

"Down past the house."

"It's on the way. You hop on up, and I'll take ya." She held out her hand to help Lizzie up, then flicked the reins. The wagon rumbled; the harness rattled; the horses neighed.

"There he is." Lizzie pointed, then called his name.

He looked up without straightening.

"I'm going to town with Molly."

He waved his hammer over his head in acknowledgment.

"I hope you don't mind my saying so, but that's a mighty interesting fence Caleb's working on." Molly shook her head. "You expecting an Indian attack or something?"

Lizzie adjusted herself on the hard bench. "Caleb likes building fences."

"I guess he must. I thought he would be eager to be in the fields, though."

"Father Hughes is plowing."

Molly turned and looked directly at her. "Mr. Hughes is plowing when Caleb is home?"

Lizzie stared down the road without answering.

"My uncle came home from the war," Molly continued. "Now I'm not one to say anything about a person's character, but my uncle is downright crazy." She shook her head. "He didn't spend one night in the house. Said it was too close. He preferred to sleep outside." She made a burring sound. "In a house he lived in all his life, mind. So he packed up a few things and left. Said he was going into the mountains where he wouldn't have to see nobody."

Lizzie was curious. "Is he still there?"

"Far as I know. When I asked Pa if he thought Uncle Clem would be back, he said there's some things a man has to work out on his own." Molly's voice thoughtful, she added, "I guess Caleb's got to work out a few things hisself, too."

Lizzie had been trying her best to avoid the subject. She met Molly's questioning gaze without flinching as she pointedly changed the subject. "Tell me about yourself. Caleb says you live west of here."

Molly studied Lizzie a moment, her expression growing hard. "I get it. Subject closed. Fine and dandy." She adjusted herself so she could put one booted foot up and lean against her leg. "I live with my pa about ten miles farther west. Right along the river."

"What about your mother?"

"My mother's dead. I don't remember her. My pa and Uncle Clem—he's the one I just told you about—they raised me best they could. Some would say it weren't none too good, but I got no complaints. I learned how to cook and clean well enough, and there ain't anything about breaking and raising horses I don't know. Nor can't do."

Lizzie laughed then. "You don't need to defend yourself to me."

"Guess I don't." She pulled the team to a stop. "Here we are at the post office. You want to mail your letter?"

"Are you going in?" She gave the building a dubious look.

Molly chuckled. "Don't you let Miss Priss get to you."

"Miss Priss?"

"Actually her name is Miss Melinda Johnson, but I always call her 'Miss Priss' cause she looks down her nose at me like I stink. I bet she said something mean and nasty to you, too."

"Accused me of stealing a man from under her nose."

Molly nodded. "Not like you see a whole lineup waiting a chance to ask her out. Don't pay her no mind."

"You're right." Lizzie jumped down from the wagon and marched inside, handed her letter to Miss Priss—Miss Johnson, she corrected herself—smiled, said, "Isn't it a pleasant day?" and sauntered back out.

"Weren't so bad, was it?" Molly asked.

"Not at all. But then I never gave her a chance to say anything." She hopped up on the wagon again. "I hope I didn't appear rude, though."

"Don't worry about it. Miss Priss would never notice unless it had something to do with a man." She guided the horses down the street. "You got something else to do, or you want to wait while I get the feed?"

"I don't mind waiting." In fact, she welcomed the chance to look around. Most times when she came to town, she got no farther than the Duncan home on the south edge. The train station lay on the east side, with the road leading directly out of town. Apart from that, the post office was the only place she'd been. She craned around, taking stock of the wide streets and board sidewalks.

Molly pulled to a stop in front of a feed store.

Down the street a spire poked skyward. "Isn't that a church?" she asked Molly.

"Yup." Molly heaved a heavy sack into the wagon.

"Then why do we meet at the Sidons'?"

Molly brushed her hair off her forehead. " 'Cause it ain't necessary to have a fancy building."

Lizzie leaned over until she could see the white frame building. It was plain as pudding compared to the fine structures back home. "I can't see that would be a problem."

Molly laughed. "Nothing very fancy about that building, I reckon. Nor the other church in town." She ducked inside the building, returning in a few minutes with a box.

Lizzie waited until Molly was back on the seat beside her before she asked, "Are you saying those people believe it's wrong to meet in a church building?"

"Not exactly wrong, I guess. Just not necessary. Now if you were to mention something fun or exciting, that would be wrong."

"You're not serious."

"Maybe I am. But I never pay it much mind. I do as I like and mind my own business. I 'spect folks to do the same for me."

"Oh, my. Caleb never said anything about this to me."

"Maybe he don't care one way or the other."

Lizzie turned to watch the girl's face. Her remark made Lizzie uneasy. "What do you mean?"

"Only that it strikes me Caleb don't put up much argument, but that don't mean he agrees with everything he's told."

Lizzie thought about his fixing the roof on Sunday; how he nodded when his mother criticized him for going to town almost every day to see Frankie, then continued to do exactly as he had done before. Even working on the fence. Both his parents had made pointed remarks about it, yet Caleb continued unperturbed. "I believe you're right."

"You betcha I am." She turned the wagon to return home. "You sure there's no place you'd like to stop? I ain't in a big hurry to get home."

"Could we stop at the Duncans'? I'd like to see how they're doing."

"Fine by me." She pulled to a halt in front of the Duncan barn. "You go on ahead and see Mrs. Duncan. I'll just have a gander around."

At the sound of the wagon, Robbie came from the interior of the barn. He called a greeting to Lizzie, and his eyes brightened as he recognized Molly. "Hey, Molly! Come and see the team you sold us."

Lizzie left Molly and Robbie to their inspection of the horses and went inside to find Pearl sitting at the table, staring blankly.

In the other room, Frankie coughed until he gagged. Lizzie shuddered.

"Pearl?"

Pearl lifted wide, desperate eyes. "I can't stand it. Every day he gets worse. I know I should be grateful for whatever time I have, and you know I am. But to listen to him struggling for breath and to see his face screwed up from the pain. . ." She shivered.

Lizzie held her, letting Pearl sob against her shoulder.

Frankie coughed again.

Pearl sighed. "Here I am a-rattlin' on about how awful

things are when I wouldn't be wanting to miss a minute." Her voice dropped, and she plucked at her fingers. "I only wish Frankie didn't have to suffer so."

"Pearl?" Frankie called, his voice barely audible. Even that little effort made him cough again.

"I'm coming." She reached for Lizzie's hand. "You'll come and say hello, won't you?"

"Of course." She looked around the room. "Where are the children?"

"Playing out back. I'm trying to keep them out of the way as much as possible."

"You can send them to me anytime you want, you know."

Pearl nodded. "I know, and I thank you. Mrs. Lawson across the street will take them for me, too."

They went to Frankie's bedside. Frankie reached for Pearl's hand, and she leaned over and kissed his brow. "Hello, Lizzie." His voice grew reedier every day. His wheeze filled the room. His face was drawn with pain.

Lizzie patted his hand. Words seemed so inadequate. She sat with Pearl and Frankie a few minutes. They didn't speak as they clung to each other, drawing strength from being together. "I have to go," she whispered.

"You'll come again soon?" Pearl asked, momentarily diverting her gaze from watching her husband.

"Bring your flute." Frankie opened his eyes for a heartbeat. Long enough for her to see the depths of his pain.

"I'll be back, and I'll bring my flute." It took all her self-control to keep her voice steady before she rushed outside and gulped in a deep breath.

Robbie and Molly leaned against the wagon talking. Molly straightened as Lizzie approached. "Ready?"

Lizzie nodded. She smiled at Robbie, trying to hide her

sadness; but from his expression, she knew he understood his father was failing. She squeezed his shoulder. "Come and get us if you need anything."

He nodded. "I will."

"Remember what I told you about the team," Molly called as they drove away.

Robbie waved. "I will."

"I told him I'd buy back the team if it helped them any. Robbie says Audie can't seem to keep both outfits going." Molly shook her head. "Beats me why he can't. There's plenty of work hauling freight around here. The man at the feed store was complaining he couldn't get anyone to take a load out to Willard's. How're Frankie and Pearl?"

Sudden, unexpected tears choked Lizzie's throat. For a moment, she couldn't speak. "They're so brave and loving." Their devotion filled her with loneliness.

"Frankie getting any better?"

Lizzie swallowed hard. "I don't think Frankie is going to get better."

Molly jerked around to face her. "He's dying?"

"He's failing badly."

Molly puffed out her cheeks. "Well, I never guessed. No one said anything." She squinted and pulled her mouth to one side. "That makes a whole lot of difference."

Lizzie drew her brows together. "To what?"

"The way Audie is neglecting their business. I thought Frankie would be on his case soon enough."

Lizzie nodded, though she only half guessed what Molly meant.

Caleb was still working on the fence when they neared the farm. Molly pulled up at the edge of the road and hopped down. "Hope you don't mind if I have a chat with your man."

Lizzie climbed down after her. "Of course I don't." She wondered if Molly would pay any attention if she'd said otherwise.

"Caleb. Something we need to talk about." Molly stood close to Caleb, her arms akimbo and her legs wide, like a fighter issuing a challenge.

Caleb straightened. He gave Molly a cautious look; then his gaze darted past Molly to meet Lizzie's eyes. She smiled, though she felt her eyes awash in sadness. The scene of Pearl and Frankie clinging together would not soon leave her thoughts.

"Lizzie here tells me Frankie isn't getting better. Maybe never."

Caleb flinched at her blunt words.

Molly plowed on. "Now there's no sense in beating around the bush. Frankie has a good freighting business, but Audie's running it into the ground. Robbie tells me he seldom has the second outfit working. What I'm wanting to know is what are you planning to do about it?"

Caleb's mouth dropped open. He blinked. "Me?"

Molly jerked her head forward. "You're his friend, right?"

Caleb nodded. "Yes."

"Then I guess it's up to you to see to his interests. Now I offered to buy back my team, but that don't make sense. What makes sense is for someone"—she poked a finger at his chest—"I'm meaning you—to tell Audie if he don't take care of things proper, he'll be answering to someone besides Robbie or Pearl." She took a deep breath. "Like you."

He scowled at her. "You done?"

She scowled right back. "You tell me. You gonna' do something?"

"I declare. Sometimes I think you should have been a man.

You bark orders like some tinhorn sergeant major."

"I'm only saying what's got to be said."

Caleb closed his eyes and sighed. "I'll go see Audie and talk to him." He glared at Molly. "Man to man."

"Fine." She spun around and marched back to the wagon. "See you, Lizzie," she called and rattled away.

"I pity the man who marries that girl," Caleb muttered.

"She's got a good heart."

"And a big mouth."

Lizzie laughed, but the sound died as her throat tightened. "Caleb, Frankie is so much worse." She flung herself into his arms. "Hold me. Just hold me."

Caleb crushed her to his chest so hard her arms hurt, but she didn't mind. Tears welled up in her throat. For the Duncans. For herself. The war had exacted a high price from everyone.

Caleb pushed her away. "I've got to go see Frankie. We need to talk."

She nodded. "I'll be here when you get back."

"I don't know how long I'll be."

"That's all right. I'll be waiting."

He searched her face hungrily, yet unsure.

She nodded. "Go now." Was he unsure of himself or her? "I'll be here."

He seemed to struggle with some uncertainty within himself before he strode away.

nine

Days passed. Lizzie accompanied Caleb to the Duncan home almost every day, playing her flute each time. Often she brought the children home for the afternoon, doing her best to amuse them and protect them from the pall hanging over their own home as Frankie worsened rapidly. But Caleb seemed more affected by Frankie's condition than the children did.

"Come to bed," Lizzie begged after a particularly trying day. She'd kept the children while the doctor came to change the dressings on Frankie's feet. Caleb had insisted on being at Frankie's side. "He needs someone to hold him when the doctor—" He couldn't go on.

"Come to bed," she said again. "You need some sleep."

"How can I sleep?" Caleb's cheeks had grown more hollow as the days passed. His eyes were lifeless, empty. "Do you think Frankie sleeps?"

Lizzie refrained from pointing out that because of drugs, Frankie slept a great part of the time. "You barely eat. You barely sleep. What help will you be to Frankie if you get sick?"

"I won't get sick," he muttered. "I never got sick during the war, and things were worse there."

"Look at you. You've lost so much weight your clothes hang."

He shrugged aside her concern.

"Come now," she begged. "You're shivering. Lie down for awhile. At least until you're warm." It wasn't cold making him shiver; it was nerves. If only he would let her comfort him, but he stiffened when she touched him. She lifted a woolen quilt from the trunk. "Here, I'll cover you with this and lie beside you."

He eyed the quilt with sudden longing and, to her surprise, let her lead him to the bedroom. He lay on the bed, covering his eyes with his arm as she pulled off his boots. He remained silent as she lay beside him and tucked the quilt around them. The tension in his body was palpable. When he started to relax, his body jerked him back to attention. Lizzie prayed, calming her own fears and worries. She prayed for Caleb and for Frankie and Pearl and their family. As her thoughts focused on God's promised care, she relaxed against Caleb, hoping he would somehow absorb her peace.

After a long while his breathing deepened, and she knew he had fallen asleep.

Even though her shoulders ached, she didn't move for fear of waking him. It wasn't until he snored softly that she cautiously shifted so she could lay her head against his shoulder and drape her arm over his chest. It felt so good to hold him. How she ached for this sort of closeness when he was awake and responding. She didn't dare think about how much he had changed. Nor what the future held for them.

Sometime during the night, Caleb shifted to his side and lay curled against her, his arm around her waist. She snuggled into his embrace. At least his subconscious mind still reached for her.

Pounding on the door jerked them awake.

Caleb leapt from bed and raced to the door.

Robbie stood in the gray light of early morning, his eyes so wide they looked white. His panting filled the silence. "Mom asked if you would come."

"I'll get my boots," Caleb said.

"Both of you," Robbie insisted.

"Give me a minute," Lizzie called from the bedroom. There was only one reason Robbie would come for them. Frankie's time had come.

She dressed faster than she ever had before. Caleb grabbed her arm, and they practically ran the whole distance to town. Robbie hadn't bothered to wait for them.

They slipped in quietly without knocking.

Pearl sat at Frankie's bedside. Robbie dropped to the floor at her feet.

Frankie reached a hand toward them. "I'm glad you could make it," he whispered.

Lizzie hugged Pearl.

Caleb pulled two chairs close, and they huddled at Frankie's side.

"I have something I want to say to you." Frankie's eyes bored into Caleb. He coughed and struggled for breath.

"You shouldn't talk," Caleb protested.

"I have to."

Caleb nodded. "I'm listening."

"All six of us signed up together. Dick got it first with a bullet from the Germans. Then August and Gustave got their lungs burned out with gas." He coughed, ending on a gasp. "I only got a little." His painful gasps made Lizzie's lungs ache.

"I thought George would make it, but we found him dead in the trench after that horrible attack." He paused again to catch his breath. "But I don't want to talk about them. I want to talk about you." He fixed Caleb with a piercing gaze. "I been thinking on this some time now so I want you to listen real good."

Caleb nodded again. "I'm listening."

"I don't want to remind you of the others except to say they died out there. At least I get to die in the loving arms of my wife. I get to see my young ones again before I go."

His voice rasped, and he stopped to cough.

Pearl leaned forward, wiping his brow. "Maybe you should rest, Dear."

Frankie patted her hand. "I'll rest in a minute."

"Caleb." Frankie pulled Caleb closer. "You're the only one left, and you been walking around with a long face like you despise your life."

Caleb didn't waver from Frankie's intense stare.

"Don't you see, Caleb? You got to make your life count for the rest of us. If you don't, it will all be for nothing. Don't you see that?"

Caleb's gaze bored into Frankie's eyes.

"You're all that's left of us. You got to be our standard-bearer. Do you understand?"

The air pulsed with Frankie's intensity. Caleb stared long and hard into his eyes. Lizzie could almost taste Caleb's resistance.

Frankie shook his arm. "Stop feeling guilty about being alive. Do you think any of us would change it? Don't you see? I'm glad you'll live on for us."

Lizzie silently prayed Caleb would respond to Frankie's words, that this would mark a turning point in his life.

The men looked at each other without blinking; then Caleb shuddered. Frankie nodded. "I know it's hard to forget. Impossible. But you must look to the future. Love that pretty little wife of yours, who is so in love with you that it hurts my eyes the way she watches you." His breathing was so tortured, he had to stop. "Love her," he whispered. "Don't shut her out. Raise a bunch of babies. Live life to the full." He closed his eyes, exhausted.

Caleb sat back, his feelings hidden behind a stiff mask.

Lizzie prayed Frankie's words would sink into Caleb's heart.

Frankie rested a moment, then opened his eyes and looked about. His gaze fell on his eldest son. "Robbie, come here."

Robbie knelt at the side of the bed. "Don't talk, Dad."

Ignoring his son's advice, Frankie cradled Robbie's head in his quivering hand. "Son, you've had a heavy load, and you've done a fine job. As good as most men could do. I'm so proud of you."

Robbie ducked his head against his father's chest. His tears soaked the worn quilt.

"You are my pride and joy. Don't ever forget how much I love you."

"I won't," Robbie said, his voice choked with tears.

The room grew quiet except for Frankie's rattling breath. Robbie lifted his head from the covers but remained leaning against his father's bed.

"I want to see the children," Frankie whispered.

Pearl nodded to Robbie, and the boy sprang to his feet to get his younger brother and sister.

Lizzie rose, reaching for Caleb, intending to give the family some privacy, but Frankie opened his eyes.

"Stay," he rasped.

They sank back to their chairs as Robbie led the two younger children to Frankie's bedside. Frankie reached for Junior.

"I want to hold him," he whispered, and Pearl lifted the boy to his side.

"Little Frankie." His father's voice was an agonizing sound. "My own little boy. I'm so glad I got to see you again." He held the child close, tears streaming down his face.

Lizzie wiped tears from her cheeks.

"Come here, Violet."

Pearl pulled Junior to her knee so the little girl could crawl up beside her father.

"My sweet Violet. You're as pretty as your mother." He choked and coughed. "I'm so proud of you." He coughed again and, unable to continue speaking, stroked his daughter's head.

Violet sobbed softly.

Pearl disentangled the child. "Robbie, take them back to their beds."

Robbie took a child in each hand, pausing at the door. "Can I come back?"

Pearl nodded. "As soon as they settle."

Frankie lay back, exhausted.

Lizzie and Caleb sat quietly keeping vigil. Pearl shifted closer, holding Frankie's hand.

Silence, like the darkness of a moonless night, settled around them, broken only by the rasping struggle of Frankie's breathing and the muted sound of Robbie slipping back into the room.

The morning sun slanted through the window, dropping a patch of warmth out of reach of those who huddled by the bed.

Violet tiptoed into the room, Junior at her heels.

Pearl hugged the children, then whispered to Robbie, "Take them across the road to Mrs. Lawson."

Frankie twitched at the barely audible sound.

Pearl turned to the younger two. "You stay with Mrs. Lawson. Daddy needs it quiet."

Violet nodded, taking Junior and leading him from the room. Robbie followed them, returning a short time later.

Frankie's breathing grew erratic. Lizzie held her own breath every time Frankie's rasping quit. Sometimes she thought her heart would explode before he gasped another shuddering breath. He opened his eyes once, seeking Pearl, smiled weakly, and again closed his eyes.

The patch of sunlight slid across the room and paused at the doorway. Frankie shuddered once. The room echoed with silence as they waited for his next breath. But Frankie had breathed his last.

Robbie stared at his father's chest.

Pearl pulled him into her arms, tears flooding her cheeks. "He's gone, Son. Gone to heaven. Free from his pain."

Robbie clung to his mother, sobbing quietly.

Caleb pushed stiffly to his feet. "I'll go get the doctor." His voice quavered.

Lizzie let the tears flow. She already missed Frankie, but she couldn't wish him back.

Pearl wiped her eyes. "We have lots to do."

ह

An honor guard of veterans, including Caleb, dressed in snappy uniforms, carried Frankie's casket to the church and sat at rigid attention on the front pew during the service.

Pearl and her children sat across from them. Friends and neighbors packed the rest of the church.

Lizzie, sitting beside Robbie, looked around the simple building. It was right Frankie should be buried from a proper church. The sunlight blazed through the window. It touched the simple pine coffin, giving it a golden glow. Lizzie took Robbie's hand and squeezed.

The children had been wonderful, letting quiet tears flow as they talked about their father.

Pearl, too, seemed to gain inner strength. "I couldn't wish him back," she told Lizzie prior to the funeral. "Not to more agony. I know there'll be some who think I'm strange, but all I can think is that I had him longer than many wives and mothers. For that I'm grateful."

It was time for Lizzie to go to the front and play her flute in memory of Frankie. She'd chosen one of his favorites, "Amazing Grace." She looked around the audience as she played, recognizing many. Mother and Father Hughes sat partway back. She watched them a minute. What did they think of her playing in public like this? But she couldn't let it bother her. She was here for Frankie's sake. For Pearl and the children.

After the service, they followed the honor guard to the little plot of ground beside the church. Violet buried her face against her mother's arm as the box lowered into the ground.

Lizzie watched Caleb. She couldn't tell what he was thinking or feeling.

She had tried to talk to him after Frankie's passing, when they'd lain in bed in the comfort of each other's arms. "What Frankie said made sense. Especially the part about a wife who loves you. I love you so much it scares me sometimes." It wasn't her love that scared her. It was the fear that he didn't return her love.

"I didn't need Frankie to tell me. I've got eyes, too, you know."

She tried to contain her own annoyance. "Then why do you act as if you neither know nor care whether I love you? Am I invisible? Or is it like Frankie said, you can't forgive yourself for surviving when the others didn't?"

Although he didn't pull away from her, he stiffened, and she knew he only remained where he was in order not to prove her argument right.

"Frankie was half out of his mind."

"Could be he was, but he still saw the truth far better than you do."

"What's that supposed to mean?"

"Frankie saw that you have to put the war behind you and get on with the business of living. Otherwise all those sacrifices the others made were for nothing."

"I didn't have any say in who died and who lived. No one asked me if I wanted the burden of proving it was worthwhile. What if I don't think it was? What if I think I didn't deserve to live any more than they deserved to die? What if it was wasted?" He pushed away and swung his legs over the side of the bed.

"But, Caleb. You can't believe that."

He pressed his fists together. "Why can't I?"

"Because it would disappoint Frankie."

He slumped over his knees. "Frankie was my best friend."

"I know. If for no other reason, you must find a way to live in a manner that would honor his memory." *For my sake, too,* she cried silently. *For me.*

"If only it were that simple. 'Forget about the past and get on with life.' " He groaned. "But I can't. I don't know how."

She had no answer for him. If Frankie couldn't give him the answers he needed, she could not, for she could only guess at the horrors he had witnessed—horrors that tore at his mind day and night. She sat beside him, clutching his arm, desperately trying to reach him physically and emotionally. "Perhaps you're wanting it to be too simple. I remember what Frankie said one day, something to the effect that when the bad times came, he blocked them out and forced himself to thank God for all the good things he had."

"You make it sound as if I'm selfish and stubborn about this."

"I have no such intention, and I'm sorry if you see it that way. I only want to help you in any way I can." She swallowed hard. "I feel as if you're wandering lost and aimless. And away from me." Her throat constricted, but she forced the words out. "I don't want to lose you."

He sighed. "Frankie told me more than once I was shutting you out. I don't mean to." He wrapped his arms around her and pulled her close. "If it weren't for you, I'm sure I would have lost my mind long ago."

"Then let me help."

"How? What can you do?"

"I don't know. Perhaps it would help if you talked about what's bothering you."

He shuddered. "I couldn't bear to put it in words."

"Then why don't you simply come to me and let me hug you, instead of turning away when I reach out to comfort you?" Her throat ached at the memory of all the times he had done exactly that.

"Is that what I do?" He sounded surprised.

"Time and again."

"I didn't realize I did." He was quiet a moment. "It's just that I feel so brittle inside, I'm afraid if anyone touches me, I'll crack into a hundred little splinters."

"You're holding me now," she pointed out. "And you're even telling me what you're feeling. Do you find it frightening?"

He pulled her closer in a warm embrace so different from the desperate way he'd clutched her in his arms the past few days. "It feels good. I don't ever want to let you go."

"You don't have to. I'll always be here."

He nuzzled her hair. "I've thought about what Frankie said. I wish I could be different, but I don't know if I can. Maybe, if I try—" He rubbed her back. "Just don't lose patience with me."

"Never," she promised. Caleb had taken a big step. Tears of joy had stung her eyes.

She pulled herself back to the present.

At that moment, Caleb lifted his head and looked around the crowd at the graveside. When he found her, his eyes darkened with pleasure. He held her gaze for a moment, his look full of promise and love. His lips lifted just enough to let her know he was all right; then he turned back to his task.

She smiled to herself, her sorrow over Frankie's death eased by the joy of Caleb's changed behavior.

The pastor made an announcement that the ladies had prepared refreshments to be served at the Duncan home, and the crowd moved down the street.

The house was too small for everyone, so people milled around outside.

"You played lovely." Mother Hughes was at her elbow.

Lizzie almost dropped her cup of tea. "I wondered if you would be offended."

Mother Hughes gave a sweet smile, though Lizzie wasn't sure if it went as far as her eyes. "Not everyone agrees with us. And it seemed fitting for Frankie. I know you played for him often."

Lizzie stared after her mother-in-law as she slipped away to speak to someone else.

"Why the shocked look?" Caleb asked at her ear.

Lizzie turned to face her husband, her answer disappearing at the warm look in his eyes.

"Come on—I have some people I want you to meet." Caleb drew her arm through his and led her toward the group of veterans. "These are the men I served with." One by one, Caleb introduced them.

Lizzie shook hands and greeted them. They were all rigidly straight men in uniforms, with matching serious expressions. Except for one, a youngish looking man with a wide grin. Caleb introduced him. "This is Carson Buttes. We fought side by side in France."

Carson grinned down at her. "So this is the young lady who sent you all those letters? You should have seen him. He read every one so often the pages eventually crumbled."

Lizzie glanced at Caleb. "He never told me that."

"No, I don't expect he would. He took a lot of teasing about it. Bet you're glad to have him home safe and sound."

She hugged Caleb's arm. "I surely am. I'm sorry you've lost another of your comrades." She addressed the whole group.

They mumbled their appreciation.

Carson sobered a moment. "Poor Frankie." Then he punched Caleb on the shoulder. "But it's good to see this old dog again. How are you doing, Caleb?"

Caleb shrugged. "All right, I guess."

Carson nodded. "Hard to fit back in, isn't it?"

"Sometimes," Caleb mumbled, shifting his weight from side to side as if the conversation made him nervous.

"But then you're one of the lucky ones."

Caleb scowled at his friend. "I don't know what you mean."

"You've got a home to come back to. A pretty wife waiting. And a job."

Several of the others murmured agreement.

Lizzie silently echoed Carson's assessment, though she wondered what he would have thought if he knew Caleb's father had planted the crop, without help from his son, while Caleb spent his days working on a fence that needed no work.

"What is your situation?" she asked.

Carson grimaced. "My pa died while I was away. Ma sold the house and moved in with my sister. There's no room for me." He shrugged. "I got no home, no job."

Caleb shifted uneasily. "How about the rest of you?"

A chorus of replies. "I've been trying for months to find

work." "My brother lets me sleep in the attic." "My fiancée decided not to wait for me."

"I had no idea." Caleb sounded confused. "I guess I never realized I had it so good."

The men fell quiet for a moment; then one said in a low voice, "It's hard to fit back in."

There was a restless silence. Lizzie realized they were uncomfortable speaking of their troubles in front of her. "Excuse me. I see someone I need to talk to." She slipped away, heading toward the house, wanting to check on Pearl and the children.

A throng of people surrounded Pearl. She met Lizzie's questioning gaze and nodded a silent signal that she was doing okay.

Lizzie slipped through to the back door and looked out at the yard full of children. She picked out Frankie Junior and Violet playing with the others. Her gaze rounded the yard, but she couldn't spot Robbie, so she edged her way toward the barn.

Molly grabbed her arm. "Who's the man with Caleb?"

"Ex-soldiers who fought with Frankie and Caleb. Have you seen Robbie?"

"Robbie's in the barn with some older boys." She planted herself in front of Lizzie, demanding complete attention. "I mean the man Caleb is in hot conversation with." Molly dragged her into the room. "See for yourself."

Caleb, Carson, and another of the veterans huddled together, talking and gesturing.

"Probably talking about the war," Lizzie said.

"Isn't he a dream boat?"

Lizzie jerked around to stare at Molly. "Caleb?"

"No, Silly. That one at his right. Look at him."

Lizzie took another look. "You must mean Carson." He

appeared ordinary enough to her, though he did have a quick smile.

"Is that his name?" Molly's eyes widened.

"Would you like to meet him?"

Molly gasped. "Would I?" She pushed Lizzie forward. "Lead on."

Giggling, Lizzie allowed herself to be manipulated through the noisy crowd to Caleb's side. Caleb smiled at her even as he listened to every word of Carson's. It had been a long time since Lizzie had seen him so animated, and she silently thanked Carson.

"Ahem." Molly pushed between Caleb and Lizzie.

Carson broke off and gaped at the girl before him.

Lizzie introduced them, allowing Caleb to fill in the names of the four others, though she was almost certain Molly never heard anything but Carson's name.

"How about some more sandwiches and tea?" Caleb asked, and the other men followed him inside.

Carson hesitated. "How about you, Molly? Would you like to see what there is to eat?"

"Sounds good to me."

Lizzie chuckled as the two wandered away, oblivious to the crowd around them.

"You coming?" Caleb called, and she hurried to catch up.

He draped his arm across her shoulder, pulling her close as they entered the house. In the press of people, Caleb pulled her closer. She smiled up at him, wishing they were in private so she could kiss him.

ten

"I'm exhausted." Caleb groaned, throwing his jacket across a hook. "I thought some of those people would never go home."

Lizzie sank into a chair and propped her feet up. "I don't know how Pearl held up so well."

Caleb stretched out on the sofa. "I wish she would have let us stay to help get the children to bed."

"Me, too, but I think they were feeling the need of being alone so they can comfort each other."

"I suppose so." He grew thoughtful. "It really changes things for them."

Lizzie nodded. Frankie's passing would leave a huge hole in their lives.

Caleb pushed to his feet. "Let's go to bed." He held a hand out to her.

In bed, wrapped in Caleb's arms, Lizzie tried to relax; but despite her tiredness, her mind remained too active. She felt the same restlessness in Caleb. "You had a good time with your comrades."

"I did. They helped me see things more clearly."

She waited, wondering what he meant.

"I truly am fortunate. I have so much. Some of these men have nothing."

She hugged him. "I'm glad you're able to see that."

He pressed his face to her head. "I'm especially blessed to have you." His voice was thick with emotion.

"Caleb, we have each other. That's the best thing."

He shuddered. "I almost forgot. Seems like I wandered

around in a fog for a long time, not able to see anything but the dreadful things of the war." He shuddered again. "From now on, I'll take one day at a time and try to put the war behind me."

She hugged him tighter, kissing his chest and neck. "Now that you've dealt with it, things will get better."

"I hope so, but sometimes things will get to me."

"One day at a time." She continued to place little kisses across his skin.

The pressure of his arms changed from desperate to gentle. He stroked her hair.

She snuggled against him. "I love you, Caleb Hughes."

He grasped her chin and tilted her head back. "I love you, too." His mouth found hers, his kiss blotting out everything but her love for him.

૨ે

The days that followed were all Lizzie had dreamed of when she thought of moving to Canada as Caleb's wife. Caleb was the man she had fallen in love with back home—full of tenderness and the joy of life. Suddenly he wanted to show her everything.

"We're going to town," he announced. "I want to have a look around."

"At what?" she asked as she hurried to join him.

"The town. I haven't taken a look at it since I got back. Not a real look." He paused. "You want to go in the buggy or walk?"

She stopped and looked at him. This was the first time he had offered to ride rather than walk. She knew how much he liked walking. No, it was more than liking it; somehow the exercise seemed to enable him to deal with his tortured thoughts, as if every thudding step could drive them farther away. "I'd be glad to walk."

Side by side, hand in hand, they headed toward town.

Several yards down the road, Caleb pulled her to a halt. "Listen to that." He tilted his head, smiling.

Lizzie listened, too. The wind hurried over the top of the grass, whispering secrets from the past. Half a dozen different types of birds called out to each other. Off in the distance, she thought she heard the sound of a horse clomping along. "What are we listening to?"

"The quiet. I've never noticed how blissfully quiet it is."

Lizzie nodded. "It is nice." She took his arm and pulled him close, grateful the thundering echoes of war were fading from his mind. "So peaceful."

He grew thoughtful. "Yes."

They stopped to see Pearl and ask how she was doing. Busy canning rhubarb, she wiped her forehead and replied, "The house is empty without Frankie. I'm grateful for the children to keep me busy."

"Where are they?"

"Violet and Frankie Junior are in their room. Someone was kind enough to give them crayons and coloring books. They're thrilled with them."

"Robbie?" Caleb asked. They both worried more about him than the other children. He had seen more of Frankie's illness, and now he had more to deal with in caring for the horses and facing Audie's indifference to the business.

Pearl nodded toward the barn. "He said something about one of the wagons needing to be cleaned out."

Caleb hurried to the barn, while Lizzie lingered to visit with Pearl, but Pearl was busy. "I'll come back later," Lizzie promised and went to find Caleb.

He was in the barn, showing Robbie how to grease the wheels properly. "They'll last forever if they're taken care of properly."

"I know." Robbie sounded upset. "I told Audie that, but he says I'm only a kid. He says he won't be taking orders from a kid."

Caleb's expression hardened. "I'll have a word with Audie." He squeezed Robbie's shoulder. "You hang in there. Things have a way of working out."

"That's what Dad always said. I try to pray about it like he said, but sometimes it's hard."

Lizzie hung back, giving Caleb a chance to speak to the boy.

"I know. Sometimes it feels like God isn't listening. But remember that it isn't God who's changed. It's us. But God finds ways to help us back to Him."

Robbie stared at Caleb. "What ways?"

"It's different for everyone, I expect."

"For you?" Robbie persisted.

Caleb's expression softened. "That's easy. Your dad and Lizzie."

"How is that?"

"Well, seeing how your dad was able to stay cheerful helped. And then he made me see how much I was missing—wasting, really." He hesitated. "I suppose you might say he gave me permission to be happy. You see, I thought I didn't deserve to be happy when he and the others had lost everything."

Robbie nodded. "And what about Lizzie?"

Caleb smiled so bright it made Lizzie blink. "It's hard not to be cheered up when someone loves you as much as Lizzie loves me." He looked up and saw her. "Here she is now. You ready to go?"

Her heart brimming, she nodded. She waited until they were back on the street before she said, "That was nice. What you said to Robbie."

"He'll be all right. He's a good kid. But handling Audie is

too much for him." And then he pointed to the house past the Duncan barn. "Mr. and Mrs. Murdock lived there when I left for the war. They were an elderly couple who came over from the old country all by themselves. I wondered why they left everything and started over at their age. Mr. Murdock was a cobbler. He made my first pair of boots." He stared at the house, once painted white, but now peeling. One shutter hung loose. The screen door lurched to one side. Lace curtains hung at the window, but the house had the lonely feel of being abandoned.

Caleb seemed to have forgotten her presence.

"What happened to them?" she asked.

He turned slowly. "They both died in the flu epidemic."

He headed down the road, pointing out houses and telling her who lived in each. They passed another silent, vacant house. "My old schoolteacher lived there."

"Did she die of the flu, too?"

He nodded. "War and the flu left a lot of families with empty chairs." He stopped at the gate of a large yellow house. "This is the Carlson house."

Her mouth dried as if she'd swallowed the desert wind. "You mean August and Gustave?" Two of the men who had died at his side.

"They were the oldest of five children. Only nineteen and twenty when they died." He struggled with his emotions. "I've never spoken to their parents. I could never face them. How do I stand in front of them with not so much as a scratch and say I saw your sons die?"

She slipped her hand into his and let him squeeze hard. "It's difficult."

"I don't know if I'll ever be able to look their mother in the eye again."

The door opened. Caleb jerked back and spun on his heel,

but the woman at the door saw him and called, "Caleb, is that you?" Her voice was thick with an accent, making her words round and musical.

Caleb turned—slowly and reluctantly. "Hello, Mrs. Carlson."

"Come in. Come in." She rushed down the steps and grabbed his arm. "I been wondering when you come by and see me. And this be your nice little wife from over there."

Lizzie introduced herself, giving Caleb time to collect his thoughts.

"Now you come have coffee and tell me everyt'ing."

She hustled them into a big warm kitchen. Blue-and-white china loaded every shelf and the plate rack circling the room. "Now you be sitting down while I pour coffee." Not only did she pour black coffee, but she also sliced huge pieces of moist raisin cake and set a serving before each of them, then shifted her chair close to Caleb. "You tell me about my boys, yah?"

Caleb's fists closed. Lizzie wrapped her fingers around one bunched-up hand. He lifted hollow, desperate eyes to her. *Don't go back inside yourself,* she begged silently. *Don't go back to your black memories.*

He held her gaze. Slowly his expression softened, and he turned his hand over so her fingers rested in his palm.

"They died brave?" Mrs. Carlson's face wrinkled with worry.

"They died very bravely. Not one word out of either of them."

She settled back in her chair. "That is good. Very good."

"You must have taught them how to take care of others. They should have been orderlies. Every time someone else got hurt, one of them was right there applying pressure to the wound and encouraging them." Caleb chuckled lightly. "They always said the same thing. 'Looks like you'll live, but if you're going to die, do it bravely without complaining.' It became our motto."

Tears flooded down Mrs. Carlson's face, but she didn't sob. "I tell them that all the time—in joke, you understand. I never think it might come true."

Caleb placed his hand over Mrs. Carlson's. "I'm sorry you lost them. They were wonderful and brave."

"Everyone lose someone in the war."

Lizzie felt Caleb stiffen. She could hear his silent protest. *Not me. Not me.* How he hated being the only one to come back without so much as a physical wound to show for his agony.

Mrs. Carlson patted his hand. "Poor Caleb. You lose all your friends. You must hurt. Here." She patted her chest.

"I be so grateful the war ended before Anton could sign up. He be set on joining his brothers. After they die, he want to take their place." She smiled at Caleb. "I am glad you tell me about them. Now I rest easy. They make me proud." She nodded slowly. "I tell their father."

Lizzie looked at Caleb out of the corner of her eye. His face was awash with relief. At least one of Caleb's demons had turned out to be a kindly welcome. If only the other dark torments of his mind could as easily be faced and conquered.

❧

Lizzie looked out the window a few days later, wondering where Caleb had gone. It was a nice sunny day, the trees swaying gently in the warm breeze. Already the crops stood several inches tall, thick and green. Even her garden reluctantly yielded erratic rows of plants, those hardy enough to break through the soddy ground.

She longed to see Caleb and went outside to locate him. No sound of hammering led her to him. In fact, he'd abandoned the fence since Frankie's funeral. She tramped past the big house, past the barn, and saw him sitting cross-legged beside the crop, staring at the tender plants with an intensity that made Lizzie slow her steps. He had made such an effort to fight himself and his memories these past few days; but knowing how much it required of him, seeing him visibly struggle, she feared something would strike too quickly, too hard and unexpected, and it would all come undone.

She approached quietly, trying to see what it was he saw, trying to guess by the set of his shoulders what he thought.

He heard her and turned with a smile.

Her breath came out in a gust at the welcome in his eyes.

"Sit by me." He patted the ground beside him and, when she lowered herself to the grassy spot, pulled her close. She snuggled into his arms, hungering for his touch. Like a greedy child offered candy for the first time in ages, she couldn't get enough. She could have been content to sit cuddled at his side without letting any questions intrude; but when he leaned his other elbow on his knee and resumed staring at the plants, she couldn't ignore it. Call it curiosity. Or trickling nervousness. But she had to know what it meant.

"What are you doing?"

He jerked around to look at her. "Wasn't aware I was doing anything. Just sitting here."

"You were staring at the crop as if you expected it to speak."

His eyes crinkled. "Oh, that. Why, I was watching it grow. See for yourself." He turned back to squint at the plants.

She twisted her mouth, doubting he was serious, but he never blinked from his concentration.

"Try it," he said, not turning his head.

She stared at the plants. Green, tender, waving in the wind, rippling like gentle waves. Like a dance of a thousand green soldiers.

He snorted.

She jerked around to look at him. His eyes brimmed with laughter.

"You're joshing me, aren't you?" she said in annoyance.

He rubbed his knuckles against her head and laughed. "If only you could see yourself."

She grunted, pushing him to the ground to tickle him. "That's what I get for believing you. Remind me not to do it again." She tickled him until he grabbed her wrists and pinned them to his chest. She lay against him, feeling the thud of his heart, listening to his chuckle rumbling in her ear. "I could lie like this forever," she murmured. "I love listening to the sound of your voice inside your chest."

"You like this, do you?" He deepened his voice so it rumbled even more.

"I love it." She lifted her face to study him. "I love you."

He freed her hands so he could pull her close and kiss her nose, her forehead, her chin, and finally her mouth.

She leaned against his chest, a palm on either side of his head. "I will never get tired of kissing you."

He sucked his lips in and leered. "Not even when I'm a gummy old man?"

She giggled, covering his mouth so she didn't have to look at him. "Maybe I'll be blind by then."

"Ow. Your elbows are sharp." He eased her off his chest and sat up, pulling her under his arm. "I was thinking."

She kissed his neck. "Of me, of course."

He paused to kiss her before he answered. "I'm always thinking of you, but I mean besides that." He shifted to a more comfortable position. "I thought I'd go talk to Pearl and offer to buy out half the freighting business."

She pulled herself up so she could see his face better.

"It's a good business. I'm sure I could make it support both families. I'd need to get both wagons working full-time again, and I thought I'd buy a truck."

She stared. "Caleb, I don't know what to say. What about drivers?"

"Drivers are no problem. Carson would come at the mention of work. And I'd keep Audie on if he pulled his weight." His eyes blazed. "Frankie talked about his dreams for the business. He hoped Robbie would be able to take over someday. In the meantime, he could go back to school regular. Just think—this way I could make sure it would happen, and Pearl would be looked after." The words practically burst from him. "We could live in the Murdock house. That way we'd be close by."

"It seems you've thought of everything."

"You aren't in agreement?"

"It's not that." She struggled to sort out the sudden whirl of thoughts. "But it's so unexpected. You're talking about moving. Leaving the farm. What about your parents? What will they say? Don't they need you here?"

He looked at the horizon. "I can't stand the thought of farming anymore. I like to see the green plants." He nodded toward the crop. "Like this. But I can't stand working in the soil." A shudder snaked down his spine. "Father must surely see that by now. He's put in the crop without my help again this year. I suppose he will continue to do so. Or he can hire help. Plenty of men would give their right arm for a chance to work here."

"You're right, of course. But I'm sure they'll be disappointed." Mother Hughes still came every day with eggs and often stopped for a cup of tea. Since Frankie's funeral, they had struck an amiable truce, avoiding subjects that made them uneasy with each other. Lizzie doubted she and her mother-in-law would ever be wonderful friends; yet there was a certain bond she cherished, if for no other reason than she was Caleb's mother.

"I'll talk to Pearl first; then if she's agreeable, I'll speak to Mother and Father. They'll just have to understand."

❧

Pearl readily agreed to Caleb's plan, but Lizzie wasn't sure Caleb's parents understood. Mother Hughes sat at Lizzie's table the day after Caleb made his announcement, for several minutes toying with her cup before she said, "He's never been the same since the war."

"It's been hard for him."

Mother Hughes nodded. "I hoped everything would go back to the way it was, but I can see that will never happen now." She sighed heavily. "I suppose I can't blame him."

Lizzie wondered if the slight emphasis on the final word was intentional. "Perhaps he would have changed even without the war. People seem to do that."

"Humph. It certainly leaves Father and me in the lurch."

"But you managed while Caleb was away."

"That was different. We didn't have a choice."

Lizzie refrained from pointing out they didn't have a choice now if Caleb did as he planned. Mother Hughes pushed heavily to her feet. "I better go see if Father needs my help."

Lizzie stared after her mother-in-law. Father Hughes had done the spring work, as far as Lizzie could tell, without Mother Hughes doing anything more helpful than washing the windows and keeping the meals ready. She shook her head. Was this sudden burden to assist nothing more than an attempt to make Lizzie, and probably Caleb, feel guilty?

But Lizzie didn't have time for pointless guilt. Things happened too quickly. Caleb arranged to rent the Murdock house from the town. Carson Buttes arrived back in town, swinging a bag in each hand.

"Let's get to work," he said after greeting Lizzie and Caleb. "Where am I going to sleep? When do I take my first load?"

"Pearl will put you up at her house." Caleb led the way. As soon as Carson had his things stowed safely in the tiny room in the back of the Duncan house, he showed Carson the barn while Lizzie stayed to visit Pearl.

"I'll be right glad to have you for a neighbor," Pearl said, pouring tea for them.

Lizzie had a good look at Pearl. Her features had grown fine with lost weight, but her expression was serene. "Are you eating properly?"

Pearl laughed. "I'm all right if that's what you're asking. I admit I miss Frankie, but then I expected I would. But when I get to feeling sorry for myself, I remember all the wonderful times we had while he was here. After the children went to bed, he talked about the future, telling me how I would have to hang on to God and trust even when I could see nothing but fog. Like a ship out on the ocean, he said. 'Never could figure out how they knew where to go when the fog rolled in, but they followed the charts and their little instruments and always got where they were supposed to.' He told me I had to be like that. I remember that when I'm feeling down, and I read my Bible, looking for help and guidance—like a ship in a thick fog."

She stared into her cup. "And I remember the other things, too." Her voice grew low. "Like the way he'd hold my hand and tell me how beautiful I was. I knew it wasn't true, but it sure made me feel good. I'm grateful for those extra times we had together."

Lizzie dashed away a tear. "You shared a wonderful love."

Pearl's smile was gentle. "One to last a lifetime. Now tell me what you have to do before you can move."

eleven

The Murdock house—her new home, Lizzie reminded herself—stood as it had the last day the Murdocks lived in it, right down to the quilts on the beds, the flour and sugar in barrels in the pantry.

"And dust enough to build a small farm," Molly said, swiping her hand over the table. She wrinkled her nose. "Phew. Didn't anyone think to empty the slop pail?" Holding her nose with one hand, she grabbed the offending bucket and dashed outside.

Lizzie opened the windows, breathing in the clean air.

"It looks like a lot of work." Caleb stood in the middle of the room, appearing for the first time as if he regretted the whole idea.

Lizzie pulled her head inside. "A little hard work is all it needs."

"And many hands make light work," Carson added.

Molly hurried in. "So enough jawing. Let's get to work. Caleb, take that silly look off your face and take down the curtains so we can wash them." She eyed Lizzie.

Lizzie jumped before Molly ordered her about. "I'm going to clean out all the cupboards and see what can be salvaged."

Molly turned to Carson. "You fetch wood and get the fire going so we can heat water."

He grinned at her without moving. "You sure are bossy for someone no bigger than a whistle."

Molly drew herself up tall, planted her hands on her hips,

and scowled at him. "You'd think you'd be used to taking orders, having been a soldier and all."

"Never took orders from no woman." His lazy smile lingered as he glanced down her length. "Though I can't say you look much like a woman dressed in trousers and a man's shirt."

Lizzie hid a smile, expecting Molly to give Carson the sharp edge of her tongue. Molly didn't take kindly to people making personal comments. More than once, Lizzie had seen her strike out when someone said something about the way she was brought up.

Molly snorted. "I can work as hard as any man. Better than some, I daresay." She swaggered closer. "Want to rassle and see who comes up on top?"

Carson's grin widened. "Another time, maybe." He flicked a strand of her hair.

Molly jerked back, sending the coppery waves over her shoulder. Her scowl deepened.

Carson's expression grew hard. "Don't try to order me about again."

Molly spun on her heel, an angry sound burring through her teeth. "Who needs your help? I'll do it myself." She flung out the door, letting it slam behind her.

Lizzie kept her head downward, but out of the corner of her eye, she watched keenly the play of emotions on Carson's face.

"Whew." He wiped his forehead. "A little spitfire, isn't she? I better help her before she gets it in her mind to set fire to my britches." He hurried out.

Caleb stared after them, his arms full of dusty curtains. "That Molly. She's nothing but a little hooligan."

Lizzie laughed. "Have you looked at her recently? She's beautiful and kind."

Caleb snorted. "I've seen her every day since she was old

enough for her father to toss into a saddle. Or at least every week at church. She's always been wild and rude. She needs breaking as much as any of her horses."

Lizzie nodded. "I think that's what scares her."

"Huh? Molly scared? Sure could have fooled me."

"She's trying to hide it, but if I don't miss my guess, she's fallen head over heels for your friend Carson."

"Carson? No. I better warn him."

She glared at him. "Don't you dare. Besides it's probably too late."

"Are you saying he's in love with Molly?" Caleb dropped the pile of curtains and moved closer to stare into Lizzie's face. "What makes you so sure of yourself? They act more like cat and dog than"—he swallowed hard as if it hurt even to think of it—"girlfriend and boyfriend. I hope the best for Carson."

"My sympathies are more with Molly. Carson sees she needs taming, and I'm thinking it might be a hard lesson for Molly to learn. Poor girl."

Caleb shook his head. "I think it's all in your imagination."

Molly flung the door open and stomped in, her arms filled with split wood. Lizzie and Caleb stared at her, then looked at each other before they scurried back to their tasks. There was no disguising the angry tempest raging inside Molly.

She slammed the pile of wood down, rattled the stove lids with unnecessary force, and mumbled, "Too big for his britches, he is. If he thinks I'm going to bow the knee to him, he's in for a big surprise."

Lizzie grinned at Caleb with an I-told-you-so nod, then pretended to be very busy pulling items from the top shelf.

Carson returned, his arms also full, a pleased grin on his face.

Lizzie saw the speculative glance he shot at Molly's back. She would have given anything to know what happened outside.

The four of them worked diligently throughout the morning, Lizzie and Caleb covertly watching the other two while Carson and Molly pointedly ignored each other.

The sun hung directly overhead, pouring added warmth to heat from the stove, when Robbie wandered in.

"Boy, you got a lot done."

Lizzie wiped her brow on the rag she held. "Almost finished the main floor except to put everything back."

Carson had rolled up the rug in the front room and taken it outside to beat, then helped Caleb haul out the furniture so he could wash the wooden chairs and, after that, beat a cloud of dust from the upholstered sofa and chair. Molly had washed all the curtains and hung them on the line. After Lizzie finished the cupboards, she had washed windows. Caleb scrubbed the floors until the bare boards gleamed, then found a ladder and washed the outside of the windows.

"Mom says to come for dinner," Robbie told her. "It's ready and waiting."

"I didn't expect her to feed us."

"She don't mind. She's so glad you're going to be close and Caleb is going to run Dad's business that I think she'd like to order a holiday."

Lizzie laughed. "I think by the time we get this place cleaned up and our stuff moved, *I'm* going to order one." She took her bucket of dirty water outside and threw it in the alley, calling to the others, "Pearl's got dinner ready for us."

They trooped past the barn to where Pearl had a long table set up in the yard.

Caleb sniffed. "I smell fried chicken."

Carson sighed. "I didn't realize how hungry I was."

Pearl and the children joined them, and they all ate the food with a zeal born of hard work.

❧

The next day the four of them finished cleaning the house from top to bottom and stood side by side in the front yard admiring their work.

"It's a nice house," Lizzie said. "I'm excited about moving in."

Caleb draped an arm around her shoulders. "We had a few days together in England. We've had a couple of months on the farm, but it seems like we'll really begin our lives together when we move here."

She nodded. "I know what you mean." Their first few months together in Canada had been less than idyllic. "I'm looking forward to beginning again."

Molly tilted her head and studied the house. "Cleans up real nice all right. Makes me wish—" She sighed without finishing.

The rest turned to look at her, but it was Carson who asked, "What do you wish for, Molly?"

She shook her head, refusing to answer.

He persisted. "A house like this, perhaps?"

She waved her hands as if to dismiss the topic. "I'm content where I am. No need to be wishing for anything more."

Lizzie watched her friend, recognizing the confusion and longing in her expression. Poor Molly. It seemed the idea of leaving her childhood home and contemplating starting her own frightened her. No doubt without a mother to train and prepare her, Molly felt out of her element. Lizzie hugged her. "When the time is right, you'll find it easier than you think."

Molly's expression hardened. "I'll not be foolish enough to leave my pa and give up my freedom." Her gaze darted toward Carson, then back to studying the house, as if even looking at the man put her whole life in jeopardy.

Carson leaned back, his arms across his chest. He watched Molly, his expression guarded. "It looks mighty nice."

Lizzie was certain he didn't mean the house.

"You need help packing up your stuff?" Molly asked.

"No, there's hardly anything, but thanks anyway. We should be moved in by tomorrow night, so come over for tea—both of you."

Carson nodded. "We'll leave you to settle in and enjoy your new home on your own." He turned to Caleb. "I'll take that order out first thing in the morning."

&

Next morning, Caleb brought some cases from the woodshed. "Will this be enough?"

"I'm sure it will. Most things will fit back into the trunks. There's only your clothing and the stuff on the bookshelf."

"Do you want some help?" He stood in the bedroom doorway, watching as she folded her clothes into the trunk.

"Do you have time? I thought you were eager to get into town and get some orders worked out."

"I am, but I have the wagon here. If it doesn't take too long for you to get everything ready, I thought I could make one trip. That would leave you most of the day to get settled in."

"You could pack the coats and boots by the door." He left a box at the foot of the bed, then turned back to the other room.

"If you have time, maybe you could empty the bookcase, too," she called after him.

She folded away the clothes, closed the trunk, and wired the lid of the crate shut, then paused to look around the room. Their first real home together—yet she had no qualms about bidding it good-bye. They had crossed through a difficult period together, and she was more than ready to get on with loving each other.

Filled with eagerness at what the future held, she hurried into the other room in search of Caleb.

He sat in the rocker, her writing things in his lap, staring straight ahead, his eyes unfocused, his cheeks drawn into dark hollows.

Her heart lurched as she hurried to his side. "Caleb, what's the matter? You look like you've seen a ghost."

He held out a sheet of paper. "What's this?"

"A letter?"

He nodded. "A letter from your father."

"Yes. I can see that. But why does that bother you? My father has written several letters."

He shoved it toward her. "Did all of them suggest you should go home?"

Her heart felt as if it were something dead. She didn't need to look at the letter to know he had found the one in which Father had offered to pay her passage home.

"How long has this been going on?" His voice sounded raspy, as though his throat were too tight.

"Nothing is going on. I got this weeks ago."

"When were you planning on telling me?"

"I don't know what you mean. You could have read the letter anytime you wanted. I've never hidden any of my letters from you."

"When were you planning on telling me you were going home?"

She gasped. "I'm not planning on going home. I wrote Father the same day and said so. This is my home. I belong with you." She reached for him, longing for him to laugh and say he was glad it was a mistake. But he shrugged away from her touch.

"I think you should go home."

She cried out as if she'd been bitten.

"Your father is right. I've changed. I'm not the man you married. Go home, Lizzie. Go back where you belong."

"No!" The cry of protest ripped through her. "I belong here with you, Caleb."

He shoved the pile of papers to the floor and jumped to his feet. "This place is no good for you. It reeks of death and war. I'm no good for you. I will always be haunted by the war. It's best you go home."

She grabbed his arm, not releasing it even when he jerked back. "I am not going home, Caleb Hughes. My home is with you. I will not leave even if you try to drive me away. I love you. You can't pretend I don't."

He kept his back to her, his arm stiff under her fingers. "I'm not saying you don't. What I'm saying is this place is not good for you."

"Perhaps you should let me be the judge of that."

Apart from the twitch beneath her palm, he gave no sign of having heard.

She scooped up the papers he'd dropped and put them in the crate. "I think everything is ready, if you'd care to load it on the wagon."

He didn't move.

"Caleb, I'm not leaving."

He shuddered.

"You can believe I'm staying because I want to, or you can believe I'm somehow forced to stay. But I will not go." She waited and, when he didn't respond, tried again, her words soft. "We've been through the worst. Let's not go back to that again." She almost said something about how would Frankie feel to see him doing this, but she wanted him to change his mind for her sake. Hers and his. She wanted him to believe in her love and find the strength to respond to it.

After what seemed an incredibly long time in which she couldn't draw a breath, he grabbed a crate and hauled it outside.

Lizzie sucked in a gush of air, letting it sweep into her pores. Love and prayer and a good deal of faith had seen Caleb over the last dark spell. She prayed it would work again.

She waited as he silently loaded the trunks and crates and drove to town, where he unloaded them with equal silence, then drove to the barn, his jaw set in a hard line, his eyes avoiding her.

Lizzie sat down on the sofa Carson had cleaned so meticulously. The house that had seemed so bright and cheerful yesterday now hid depressing shadows. She shivered. She must not let Caleb's dark mood affect her so she couldn't function. She forced herself to unpack, even though her insides echoed with loneliness.

As soon as the clothes were hung in the closet and the bed made with fresh sheets, Lizzie put her Bible and writing materials on the shelf next to the sofa, where she could look out toward the barn. She poured tea and sat down to read her Bible and pray, feeling as never before the need for God's strength and intervention in this situation.

Caleb came out of the barn, Robbie at his heels, and glanced toward the house. Lizzie couldn't be certain if he saw her in the window, but he paused, his expression thoughtful, and stared in her direction.

"Caleb, I love you," she whispered. "Please don't shut me out or go back to your dark memories." She took out her flute and began to play, able at last to play in her own home.

She had no notion of how long she played until she opened her eyes, surprised at how dark it had grown. But the clock read only four o'clock. She glanced out the window. The sky rolled and boiled with dark clouds, and her insides turned to ice. In Caleb's present state, a thunderstorm could send him back into the dark pit of his mind.

There had been one noisy storm since Frankie's funeral. Caleb had shivered in the rocker. When she hurried to his side, he had pulled her to his lap and buried his face against her. "I will never be able to hear thunder without thinking it's German guns."

"I wish I knew how to help you." She ached so much at his distress that she felt as if she'd been run over by wild horses.

"I wish I could erase my mind."

"Would it help if I played for you?"

His shivering stopped for a moment. "It seems silly to be so upset. We need the rain. I know we do. Yet I hate it. All I can think of when it rains is being cold and wet and muddy. Endless seas of mud."

She hugged him close, crooning as one would to a baby, loving that he would allow her to comfort him this way.

"Maybe music would help," he murmured.

She hurried to get her flute, and as she played Brahms, he slowly relaxed, closing his eyes and leaning his head back. She could only guess what was going on in his mind; but she imagined that in concentrating on the music, he blocked out the sound of the storm—or at least the vicious memories it brought. She hoped the storm also kept her music from reaching the big house; but if it didn't, she would face whatever criticism Mother Hughes levelled at her. Right now all that mattered was helping Caleb fight his inner battle.

After awhile, the thunder had passed, and the rain drummed softly on the roof, like a gentle marching. Caleb had opened his eyes and looked toward the door.

She broke off playing, waiting, wondering.

He took a deep breath and pushed to his feet, his fists clenched at his sides. With purposeful steps, he strode to the door and threw it open, letting in the damp, fresh air.

Lizzie had hurried to his side, slipping under his arm.

"I must face it and convince myself it's benevolent." He sounded as if he had his teeth gritted together.

"A gift from God," she whispered.

"Yes. 'He prepareth rain for the earth and maketh the grass to grow.' I think that's in the Bible somewhere, but don't ask me to prove it." His voice filled with wonder as if discovering for the first time the blessing of rain.

She hoped he had at last conquered his fear of thunder and rain in that last storm, but now she feared the worst. She prayed for God's intervention; but unable to stand looking out the window and wondering, she hurried outside and found Caleb and Robbie in the barn, examining a rack of harnesses. She held back, not wanting Caleb to guess she was worried.

Robbie saw her, though. "Caleb's been showing me how to clean all this stuff up so we can use it again. Dad planned to teach me, but—"

Lizzie touched the boy's shoulder. "Your dad would be so happy someone is teaching you the things he wanted to."

Robbie brightened. "He would, wouldn't he?"

Lizzie lifted her gaze to Caleb and caught the startled look in his eyes before he let his glance slide past her.

"Are Audie and Carson both out?"

Robbie answered her. "Yup. And Caleb says he thinks there's enough work for another outfit. He says maybe we'll go look at a truck. Isn't that right, Caleb?"

"Yup."

Lizzie couldn't help but be pleased at Robbie's excitement.

"I'm sure your dad would be happy." She meant the words for Caleb as much as for Robbie. Frankie would not want any of them to waste one minute of life.

She listened to Robbie explaining his work and his plans for the future. "What about school?"

He wrinkled his nose. "I have until September." He shrugged and gave her a mischievous grin. "Maybe by then there'll be so much work, I'll have to help."

Caleb hung some leather straps over a nail, his back to them. "There'll never be too much work for you to quit going to school."

Robbie sighed. "I know."

Lizzie laughed. "I better go back and put potatoes on. You'll be in for supper, Caleb?" She fully expected he would be, yet she longed for some sort of acknowledgment from him.

"Yup." His gaze flicked over her; but at least he had answered, and she hurried to the house, casting an anxious glance at the sky. The clouds twisted like a windblown rag caught on the fence, but the black thunderclouds stayed to the west. Perhaps the storm would pass them by.

The storm still held at bay when Caleb came in for tea—supper, Lizzie corrected herself. He seated himself at the table and responded to her questions with monosyllabic answers.

Finally she plunked down in her chair, facing him. "Caleb, I don't know why you're unhappy with me. I've done nothing different. Certainly nothing to make you angry. This whole thing has gone on long enough, so far as I'm concerned. When Frankie died, you promised you wouldn't waste your life living in the past, yet it seems you're more than ready to do just that. And for what? A letter I've already explained carries no threat or secret." She waited, and when he stubbornly kept his gaze fastened on his now-empty plate, she sighed. "I can't help wishing you cared enough about me to make me the same promise you made Frankie."

She bit the inside of her lip. If she'd hoped to prod him into some sort of response, she failed. His fists tightened—the only indication he even heard.

And as if to prove the futility of trying to reach him, a flash of lightning brightened the room. Caleb's chair crashed to the floor as he leapt to his feet. He looked around wildly as if seeking someplace to hide; but before he could decide where to go, thunder crashed through the room.

He fled into the front room and huddled on the sofa as the storm kicked and spat out bolt after bolt of lightning, clap after clap of thunder. Rain slashed against the windows like tiny knives. Then the storm passed, leaving only the driving rain.

"The mud!" Caleb rushed out the back door into the rain, Lizzie at his heels.

"Caleb, what are you doing?" She raced after him into the barn. In the gloom, he grabbed a bundle and turned on his heel, rushing past her, back out into the rain. He hurried down the alley, ignoring her call. Water dripping down her face, she hurried after him. Anyone seeing them would have thought they'd lost their minds. No hats. No jackets. She probably looked as bedraggled as she felt, running to keep pace with Caleb.

They raced down the alley, past the feed store where Lizzie glimpsed someone bent over a table next to a lighted lantern, past the church where the wind moaned through the steeple, sending shivers racing up and down her spine, raising a crop of goose bumps on her arms.

Caleb yanked open the gate next to the church and hurried into the graveyard.

Lizzie ground to a halt.

Trees lined the back of the yard. Rain rattled on the leaves.

Shivering violently now, she stepped through the gate, looking around for Caleb. She found him at Frankie's grave, now marked with a simple wooden cross.

"I've got to cover him before he gets muddy." He threw the bundle on the ground and unfolded a canvas tarp. "Help me," he begged.

She grabbed a corner and helped him tug the canvas over the fresh mound, covering the bare dirt. "The wind will blow it off," she said.

"I brought spikes." He pulled a hammer from his back pocket and drove long, wicked-looking spikes through the canvas into the grass. Satisfied at last, he stood back. "It's all I can do, Frankie. Take care."

Lizzie wiped her muddy hands on her skirt. The mud clung.

"Let's go home," Caleb said, taking her arm.

The rain continued all the way home. Lizzie shivered. She was soaked to the skin, muddy and miserable. *This is what they put up with day after day. Night after night.* For the first time, to a tiny degree, she understood how Caleb felt.

They stepped inside the back door.

"Wait here while I get some water," Lizzie said, slipping out of her wet shoes and dress. She grabbed a chair for him and gathered up towels. She was thankful the kettle was full of warm water. She filled a basin, washed her own hands quickly, and returned to his side, leaving the lantern on the table so they sat in dim light.

"Let me help with your boots." She loosened the laces and eased them off his feet, setting them to one side. They needed a good cleaning, but that would come later. "Now your shirt." She slipped it off, then persuaded him to shed his dripping trousers. He sank back to the chair, his hands hanging between his knees, his chin almost touching his chest. She dipped the cloth in warm water and, tipping his head back, gently wiped the muddy streaks from his face. She rinsed the cloth and tenderly washed each hand, lovingly cleaning between each finger. He watched with as much detachment as if she held the limbs of a tree.

She towelled his hair and rubbed his chest and back, trying to stimulate a spark of warmth. He didn't shiver, yet he felt so cold to her touch. She dried his legs and feet, then urged him to stand. "Come on." She drew him after her, up the stairs to their bed, where she pulled back the covers, indicating he should crawl in. Like a child, he obeyed. She slipped in beside him, cradling him in her arms, rubbing his arms and back, his coldness frightening her.

Her arms ached from the cold.

He shifted and slipped his arms around her. Suddenly their roles reversed as he rubbed her back and kissed her hair. The warmth between them flamed. He touched her chin and tilted her head back so he could kiss her.

That night they lay in each other's arms, the same spark and passion they'd shared in England now evident once again in their lives.

"I had to do it," Caleb said, his voice muffled against her hair. He kissed the top of her head. "I had to go to Frankie's grave."

She waited for him to explain.

"I couldn't leave him lying in the mud."

"I think I understand." She ached to ask where he was mentally—looking back or looking forward. More than anything, she wanted him to say the future belonged to the two of them.

twelve

Lizzie lay content in Caleb's arms.

"I've been pigheaded, haven't I?" His voice rumbled against her ear.

For a minute she didn't move, wishing they could always be like this, wrapped in each other's arms, his voice growling in her ear. But he waited for her to answer him.

"In what way?"

He chuckled. "How many ways are there?"

She pressed her palm to his chest. "How many ways are there to love?" She'd rather talk about that.

He covered her hand with his own. "Maybe only one."

She looked into his face. In the darkness, she could see only sharp angles, and she sighed, wanting to see his eyes. "One?"

"One. One way only. Forever and always with my whole heart."

She pressed her lips together and swallowed hard. "Caleb, that is so beautiful." Forever and always. What more could she ask for?

"I promised Frankie I would look forward, not back. For a little while I forgot." He hugged her tight. "I'm glad you didn't listen to me and go back to your father."

"I told you. I will not leave you." If only he would look to the future for her sake, not Frankie's; but at least he planned to take her with him into the future. Forever and always.

❧

Molly barged through the door. "You by yourself?"

149

Lizzie looked up from shaping loaves of bread. "I'm all alone. Come in. Sit down while I finish this, and then I'll make tea."

But Molly paced, pausing each time she passed the window to stare out toward the barn. "I suppose Carson is out on a run."

"He left early this morning. Caleb doesn't expect him back until almost dark. Why?"

"Oh, that man makes me so mad I could spit. He's so high-and-mighty. I told him to come for supper last night, but did he show up? No. Didn't even bother to let me know. I sat there half the night, waiting. Pa said if I figured to get that man to take to rein like one of my horses, I best be forgettin' it. 'Get yerself another bronc to break,' he says." She snorted. "I don't know who to be maddest at, Pa or Carson."

Lizzie washed her hands and poured the tea. "You and Carson seem to have picked a rocky path."

Molly dropped to the nearest chair. "He says I'm way too bossy. Well, I can't help it. I ain't never been a fancy lady. And I don't exactly like the idea."

"Is that what Carson wants? For you to be a fancy lady? Carson doesn't strike me as the sort who would care."

Molly threw her hands in the air. "How do I know what he wants? Seems every time I try to be what he wants, he up and changes his mind. I just can't get ahead of his ideas." Suddenly she leaned close to Lizzie. "How do you know if you're in love? Does it feel awful like this?"

Lizzie remembered some of the painful times with Caleb. Yes, it hurt sometimes, but she decided Molly already knew enough about that. "I guess love means you're willing to be with someone forever and always no matter what that entails. I know I'd rather put up with Caleb's moods than be parted from him."

Molly's eyes narrowed. "You saying being in love means it hurts like being whipped with wet rawhide, but it still feels better than not being whipped?"

Lizzie laughed. "I don't think that's what I mean at all. You and Carson must have some pretty fierce arguments."

Molly slumped over the table. "I guess I'm pretty set in my ways. But I'm trying to change. Trouble is, he never seems happy even when I change."

Molly's words troubled Lizzie. "Molly, you're a fun, kind person just the way you are. Why would you want to change?"

"I am?"

"Of course you are. Otherwise, why would I have you for a friend?"

"You don't think I should try to be a fancy lady?"

"Molly, you can't be someone you're not. Though I suppose you could learn new things. Like I learned to make bread."

Molly thought about that a few minutes. "I suppose if you like me the way I am, Carson should be able to."

Lizzie laughed. Suddenly she understood something about Molly. "It isn't having to change that bothers you, is it? It's letting someone else have the right to ask certain things of you. You're afraid of giving up the right to be entirely independent."

Molly hung her head. "Even Pa don't try to tell me what to do."

"I guess that's what love is: trusting someone else enough to know he isn't going to boss you around simply to prove he's boss. But it's also letting the other person make choices sometimes for the both of you." Lizzie frowned. "I don't know if I'm saying this very well. Maybe you have to sort it out for yourself."

Molly nodded, her face awash in misery. "I ain't ever trusted anyone but me."

"Love means trusting the other person—not suspiciously, like you're always expecting him to do you harm, but openly, knowing he holds you gently in his hand."

"It goes against my grain."

Lizzie silently agreed. Carson had a rough road ahead if he thought to half tame this girl. Somehow she suspected he didn't want to tame her as much as he wanted her to trust him.

❧

Audie had decided he needed some days off, so Caleb ran one wagon. The work appeared to please him, for he grew more relaxed with each day.

But for Lizzie, the days dragged by. She tried to keep busy. She played her flute for long periods at a time. Several neighbors mentioned how much they enjoyed hearing her. But boredom set in with a vengeance one afternoon, and she wandered over to visit Pearl.

Pearl stood in the middle of the room where Frankie had spent his last days. Toys and books still rested on every surface. Frankie's bed looked strangely empty. Lizzie had trouble looking at it without feeling a hollowness in the pit of her stomach.

"Where's Petey?" she asked, noticing the mouse cage was gone.

"I got Violet to take him outside. I told her it would be kind to let him go free again. I expect she'll let him go when she's ready."

Pearl stood looking at the empty bed.

"Are you all right?"

"Hmm? Oh, yes. I'm just thinking it's about time I took down Frankie's bed and put away his stuff. I'd like to turn this room back into a parlor. It bothers me to keep it like a sickroom. It's just, well, I hate to do it with the children around, you know. I don't know if I'm more concerned they might not understand or if I'm wanting to be selfish and say my good-bye without having to hide my crying."

"Why don't I take them on a picnic? We could go down to the creek. I'm bored to death with my own company, so it would be a real treat for me."

"Oh, would you? I'll make a nice lunch for you." She hurried to the kitchen. "Lots of bread and syrup and some molasses cookies. Robbie can carry a jar of water." She sliced and buttered bread as she talked.

"I'll go collect the children."

Lizzie went outside and called to them. "How would you like to go on a picnic?"

Violet jumped up. "Right now?"

"As soon as you're ready."

They found Robbie in the barn, balanced on a gate, swinging back and forth.

Violet jumped on the gate and swung back and forth with him. "Lizzie's taking us on a picnic."

"To the creek," Junior added.

Robbie kicked the wall, swinging the gate back into place, then hopped down. "Great. There's nothing to do here." He gave Lizzie a mournful look. "Caleb wouldn't take me with him."

Lizzie smiled. He and Caleb had an ongoing argument; Robbie wanted to go on every trip, but Caleb would only allow him to go on the shorter hauls, saying the longer trips were too tiring.

"I wouldn't be bored," he told Lizzie now. "I know I wouldn't."

Lizzie led the way back to the house to pick up the lunch. "Maybe he'll take you next time." Caleb had hinted he might consider it.

The four of them headed down the street. Junior ran ahead a few steps, then squatted down, his seat resting on his heels as he turned over a rock and laughed when the exposed bugs scuttled away. Then he jumped up and ran a few more steps to another rock and another family of unsuspecting bugs.

Violet skipped along, raising a puff of dust with each step so her feet seemed lost—almost suspended in earth-colored fog. She paused each time her younger brother stopped to tip over a rock, but her feet continued to move, like a marionette held by a nervous puppeteer.

Lizzie and Robbie followed more sedately, she with the bulky picnic basket in one hand, he with the jug of water.

"Caleb says he might go to Calgary and look for a truck," Robbie announced. "He thinks he might take me along."

"To Calgary?"

"Yup."

"When is he planning to go?" He'd talked about getting a truck, but he hadn't mentioned Calgary.

"Do you think Caleb would teach me to drive the truck?"

"I can't say. Have you talked to him about it?"

Robbie ducked his head. "I was afraid he would tell me I'm too young."

She studied the boy. Sometimes she forgot how young he was. The war had forced him to be a man before his time. And now his father's death had thrust more responsibility on him, even though Caleb had taken over the running of the freight business. "He hopes you'll take your father's place when you're older, so my guess is he'll be wanting you to learn as much as you can."

Robbie nodded. "But he says I have to go to school and get my book learning, too."

"I think that's a wonderful idea." If Frankie could see how

Caleb had slid into the role of mentor for Robbie, she knew he would be pleased.

She should be pleased, too, at how well Caleb seemed. He obviously enjoyed his work. He had dreams for the future. He talked of expanding the business.

She stared at the toes of her shoes as she walked, trying to ignore the burn of annoyance at the back of her throat. If only he wasn't doing it all for Frankie.

"Frankie talked of doing this." "Frankie would approve." "If only Frankie could see Robbie." She was sick of hearing Caleb talk of nothing else. She hated to admit her selfishness, but she wanted Caleb to look at her and see his future with her as the center.

"There's a nice bunch of trees," Robbie said.

She nodded. "Let's put our things there." Guilt made her voice tight. She had no right to resent Caleb's focus. She set the basket in the shade. The children gathered round her. "Let's play tag. You're it." She touched Violet's shoulder and darted away.

Violet lunged at Robbie before he could escape. "You're it."

They raced after each other until Lizzie called, "Enough. I'm so hot I think I'm going to melt. Let's get cooled off."

They traipsed down to the creek. Somewhere Lizzie had read the words "babbling brook," but this brown stream barely whispered as it slowly, reluctantly moved along. Foul-smelling mud holes dotted the banks.

"Phew." Violet held her nose.

They hurried along until they found a spot where clumps of grass had replaced the mud holes they'd seen earlier.

"Can we go wading?" Violet asked.

"I don't see why not."

The children quickly pulled off their shoes and stockings.

"Come on, Lizzie. It's nice and warm," Violet called.

Lizzie needed no second invitation and joined them. The water was surprisingly warm. Mud oozed between her toes. Schools of little minnows darted through the water, like slivers of trapped moonlight.

Junior tried to cup them in his fingers, but they darted away, in unison, like one fish held together with invisible threads.

"Magic," he said.

Robbie finally led them from the water, announcing, "I'm hungry. Let's eat."

The syrup sandwiches were sweet and satisfying. They ate every crumb and drank every drop of water, then lay on their backs. Gray-capped clouds sailed across the sky.

"It's a train," Junior said, pointing at a cloud.

"No, it's a dog," Violet insisted.

Lizzie said she saw a flower. Robbie said it looked more like a horse. A black cloud raced behind the others, making the white ones luminescent. "Ohh. That's pretty," Violet said.

Lizzie agreed. She could lie staring into the sky for hours, pretending, letting her thoughts drift, but Robbie jumped up. "Let's play follow-the-leader. I'll be it first."

He led them along a narrow cow trail, down to the creek, where they had to jump from clump of grass to clump of grass, balancing precariously. He found a huddle of rocks, as if the ground had had a giant fit of hiccoughs. Lizzie gave Junior a boost up to the first one. Robbie skipped back and forth from one boulder to another, going higher each time.

"Be careful," Lizzie begged. "Violet and Junior might fall." Junior missed the rock he jumped for. She caught him, pushing him to safety, but unbalanced, she slipped. Her palms scraped along the rough surface. Her knee banged into a sharp corner, and she yelped. One foot caught between two rocks. She lay back, gasping.

"Are you hurt?" Robbie peered down at her.

She took a steadying breath. She couldn't cry in front of the children. The nausea in her stomach subsided, and she tried to move. "I seem to be stuck."

Robbie hopped down and had a look at her foot. "Hang on. I'll push your foot out."

She winced as he grabbed her around the ankle, then bit her lip to keep from crying out as he jerked her leg. At first her foot resisted, then came free with a searing pain. Tears burned her eyes. She buried her face in her arms as she took deep breaths, uncertain if she would throw up or pass out.

"Lizzie?" Robbie touched her shoulder.

She nodded. "I'm all right." *I think.* "Give me a minute." She edged herself around to sit on the rock and stared at her foot, scraped raw and already swelling. "Help me walk."

Robbie held her arm, but when she tried to put weight on her foot, she cried out and almost fell.

Violet and Junior started crying.

"Be quiet," Robbie ordered. They obeyed instantly, Junior's eyes wide and scared. Silent tears slid down Violet's cheeks.

Lizzie gritted her teeth and scuttled along on her seat until she found a tree sturdy enough to pull herself up with. She stood one legged. A cold shiver snaked across her shoulders. The sun hid behind a cloud. She glanced at the sky. Black, angry clouds stacked in rolling waves. "We have to hurry. It's going to rain." She leaned on Robbie and tried to walk; but even placing most of her weight on the boy, she could not use the injured foot. She tried hopping. "This will take forever." She cast a glance at the churning sky and made up her mind. "Robbie, you take the children home. I'll come along at my own rate."

Violet let out a wail, then at Robbie's stern look, clamped her mouth shut.

"I can't do that," Robbie protested.

"There's no point in all of us getting soaked. Besides, your mother will worry." She forced a smile to her lips. "It won't hurt me to get a little wet. Now go on. And don't worry about me. I mean it. I'll get there by and by."

"Wait a minute." Robbie dashed to the trees where they'd had their picnic and returned with a sturdy branch. "This will help."

"Thank you. You're a good boy. Now do as I say."

He nodded. "I guess you're right. I'll come back as soon as I can."

"You don't need to. I'm sure I'll be fine." In an effort to prove her point, she took three painful steps, leaning heavily on the branch he'd given her. "See." Her ankle felt as if it were going to explode. She hoped he wouldn't guess how difficult it was not to scream with the pain.

"Come on." Robbie took the others and led them away. They glanced back over their shoulders frequently until they disappeared over the crest of a hill.

As soon as they were gone, Lizzie sank to the ground, groaning.

The wind came up, blowing through her thin clothes. Already she could taste the dampness in the air, and she forced herself to her feet. Gritting her teeth, she took another step. And another. She had to keep moving. Each step sent a shudder of pain up her leg with an accompanying wave of dizziness. One more step, she insisted. One more.

The rain began with a few cold drops; then the skies opened and drenched her. Her hair clung to her face. She licked the water from her lips and paused to wipe her eyes. She should have told Robbie to find someone with a wagon to fetch her, but it was too late now. Robbie had gone with instructions not to come back after her. She'd promised him she'd make it. Hop. Move stick forward. Hop. Wait for dizziness to pass. Hop. Move stick. Wait. Hop. Feel sick. Hop.

She let herself think of nothing else. Keep moving. Inch by inch. Move. Move. Ignore the pain. Ignore the water dripping into her eyes. Hop. Hop. Hop.

Lightning streaked across the horizon. Thunder rumbled in the distance.

Hop. Her foot slipped in the mud, and she crashed to the ground.

thirteen

She wiped her face and spit out mud. The sky was black from horizon to horizon, giving her no hope for a quick end to the storm. She lay on the wet ground. Despair soaked her bones.

Would Caleb be home yet? She groaned and sat up. Even if Caleb had returned, he would not venture out in this storm to rescue her. Only one thing had ever led him out in the rain— Frankie. The time he had covered Frankie's grave. She could imagine nothing else that would send him into the rain and mud.

She groped around for her stick and pulled it from the mud. It had snapped when she fell. She'd have to manage without it.

She scrambled up, balancing on her good leg, determined to continue. She hopped, grimacing as pain raced through her body. *It's only my leg. Why should my whole body hurt?* She hopped again, tottered, and pressed her injured foot to the ground to steady herself. The pain drove her to her knees. Without anyone to see or hear, she moaned and sobbed. "Caleb!" she screamed into the wind. "Caleb!" But Caleb couldn't hear her. He wouldn't come for her in the rain. She crawled forward on her knees, crying out when she knelt on a sharp rock. Her palms grew tender from the gravel, but she crept forward, sobbing softly.

The ground grew slippery with rain and mud. The hill seemed steeper than she recalled. Only by clutching at the tufts of grass could she make any progress. Finally, her arms shaking, she made it to the crest of the hill and, closing her eyes, lay down on the soaking grass to rest.

"Lizzie." Caleb's voice floated above her head.

She knew it was only a dream and kept her eyes closed, wanting it to last as long as possible. She wondered vaguely about the golden glow behind her eyelids.

"Lizzie." The voice was more insistent. A hand shook her gently.

She jerked her eyes open, blinking at the light before her.

"Thank God. You scared me."

"I'm hallucinating," she mumbled, closing her eyes.

"Here, Robbie—you take the lantern."

Strong arms lifted her. She opened her eyes again to squint at the face close to her. "Caleb?"

"Let's get you home."

"I didn't expect you to come." Her tongue refused to work properly.

He stumbled and she moaned.

"Hang on. We're almost there."

She gritted her teeth against the pain as he carried her to a wagon, then climbed up beside her, pulling her to his lap.

"Drive carefully, Robbie," he said.

His arms held her firm as they rattled away. A few minutes later, the wagon rumbled to a halt. Robbie jumped down and held the lantern high as Caleb carried her into the house and settled her on a chair. "Thank you, Robbie," Caleb said. "Would you mind fetching the doctor?"

"Thank you, Robbie," Lizzie mumbled.

"Yes, Sir." The boy raced away.

"Now let's get you cleaned up." He lifted her wooden arms, pulled off her sodden dress, and wrapped a blanket around her. He tenderly removed her shoes and stockings. She moaned as he touched the injured foot.

"I'm sorry, Love," he murmured.

He gently washed her face and towelled her hair. Then with a touch as soft as a cloud, he cleaned her hands and knees. Finished, he picked her up and carried her upstairs to their bed. He found her warmest flannel nightgown and pulled it over her head, then covered her with a quilt and held her close.

A knock sounded downstairs. He eased away. "I'll bring the doctor up."

The doctor examined the injured ankle. "Nothing broken as far as I can tell," he decided. "Keep it elevated for several days and stay off it."

Caleb saw him out, then came back to lie beside her, holding her close. Warmth seeped back into her bones. The pain focused in her ankle, throbbing incessantly.

"I didn't expect you to come," she murmured, relaxed in his arms.

"Why not?"

"It was raining. You hate rain. Only time you've ever faced the rain was to cover Frankie's grave."

"Do you think the rain mattered when I knew you needed me?" His voice held a sharp note, but she couldn't tell if it was surprise or annoyance.

"But I've always needed you."

"What are you trying to say?"

"I'm not a comrade-at-arms. I haven't fought beside you in the trenches of France. I'm not sick or dying." She groaned as her ankle reminded her of her injury. "My ankle will mend in a few days. But I love you, Caleb Hughes. I need to know that's important to you."

His voice grew soft. "Have I led you to believe otherwise?"

She nodded. "Sometimes. I feel petty saying this, but sometimes I feel I can't compete with Frankie."

When he would have shifted away, she held him close. "I don't mean to be demanding, but sometimes I long for you to treat our relationship with the same devotion and fervor you apply to improving Frankie's business."

He sighed.

"Have I said too much? Am I asking too much?"

"No, you're not. I honestly didn't realize how you might look at things. But tonight, when I thought of you hurt and alone out in the dark, I didn't have to think twice about going to get you." He turned on his side, holding her tight. "I couldn't live without you, Lizzie. Don't ever leave me. Don't give up on me. I love you so much it hurts."

She pressed feathery kisses to his arm where it lay across her chest. "You know I will never leave you." His words of love were all she cared about. "I love you far too much to think of life without you."

&

Ensconced on the sofa, Lizzie did not lack for company. Violet had appointed herself personal maid, hovering at Lizzie's side, wanting to do something, anything, for her.

"You want more water?"

Lizzie looked at the glass at her elbow. She'd barely had a chance to swallow a mouthful. "Not yet, Dear." Violet's face fell. "But if you get my flute, I could play awhile." The child raced to do her bidding.

Lizzie took the instrument. "I'll be all right for a bit if you want to go outside."

Violet hung back, and then her face brightened. "I'll go get you some flowers."

Lizzie longed to rest, but she knew if the child didn't hear the flute, she would come back to see what was the matter. So she played for several minutes, then let her head fall back, closing her eyes.

A knock sounded on the front door.

Lizzie sighed. Rest seemed a rare commodity around here. "Come in," she called, gaping as Mother Hughes hustled in, carrying a pot, a basket of eggs, and a loaf of fresh bread. "I brought some soup and bread."

"Why, thank you. Go ahead and put them in the kitchen. I'm sorry I can't get up."

"You stay right there. I'll look after myself."

A stove lid banged. The cupboard door squeaked. A few minutes later, Mother Hughes returned, carrying two teacups.

"I know how much you like tea."

Lizzie graciously accepted the offering, knowing if she drank any more, she would begin to float.

"It's too bad about your ankle."

Lizzie nodded. "A bit of foolishness on my part." She might as well say it before her mother-in-law did.

"It could happen to anyone."

Lizzie almost choked on her tea. She swallowed hard and wiped her eyes. "I'm not used to drinking while lying down." Never mind that she sat propped against a pile of pillows. "How are things on the farm?"

She hadn't seen Mother Hughes in days. On Sunday, Caleb had announced that since they were living in town and the church was only a hop, skip, and a jump away, they would go there rather than out to the Sidons' house to join his parents. He could have knocked her over with a feather. He'd grinned at her and added, "Besides, I like the music. Guess I got spoiled at your home."

Pleased at his admission, she gladly joined the worshippers at the little church where Frankie's funeral had been held. Her only regrets were she wouldn't see Molly so often and Caleb's parents might be hurt by the move.

"The crops are looking real good," Mother Hughes said. "That last rain came just in time. And I have a lovely garden. The flowers you planted around the house are bursting into bloom." Mother Hughes toyed with the handle of her cup. "I was wondering if you wanted me to dig them up and bring them to you."

"What a lovely thought." Lizzie considered the idea. "But, you know, I think it would be best to leave them until fall, and then I'll collect seeds from them and start them here next spring. In the meantime you enjoy them for me."

Mother Hughes looked shocked at the idea.

Lizzie smiled. "No point in letting God's gifts go to waste."

The older woman blinked, then slowly nodded. "I suppose not." She took the empty cups. "Now I don't want to tire you. I'll rinse these and be on my way."

Lizzie managed to doze a few minutes before a neighbor-lady came, bearing a freshly baked pie. Two more ladies came with gifts; then Violet burst in, her hands full of wild-flowers. She found a vase for them and set it where Lizzie could see them. "To cheer you up," she said.

"Thank you, Violet. That's sweet of you."

By the time Caleb came in for supper, she didn't know whether to laugh or cry.

"I never knew people were so kind. I've had a steady stream of well-wishers, all bearing gifts." She waved Caleb to the kitchen. "Help yourself. We'll be eating for days on what they brought."

He fixed her a plate of food and brought it to her, pulling a chair close to her side. "You've kept your foot up, haven't you?"

She laughed. "Violet guarded me all day."

He took her hand and squeezed it. "Good. I want you to

take it easy until that ankle heals."

At bedtime, he carried her upstairs to bed. "I can't imagine life without you even though I know I don't deserve you."

She pressed his palm to her lips. "You're stuck with me whether you deserve it or not."

ð€

Molly came the next day and paced from room to room.

"Please, Molly, sit down and relax."

"I'm relaxed." She perched on the edge of a chair. "Your ankle hurt much?"

"Not as bad as it did. I'll be up in a few days."

Molly bounced from her chair and stared out the front door. "How do you like living in town?"

"Fine. Why?" She suspected Molly had more than a polite reason for asking.

"Don't you miss the farm?"

"Not really. But remember, I've always lived in town. One much larger than this."

Molly turned slowly. "I've always lived in the back of beyond, where no one ever comes calling except the wind."

Lizzie watched her expression change from worry to humor.

"I remember once a preacher-man came calling. Pa and Uncle Clem stood staring at him with their mouths hanging open. The poor man stood in the open doorway and visited for about half an hour." She giggled. "After he left, Pa turned to Uncle Clem. 'Wasn't we supposed to ask him in or something?' Uncle Clem looked like he'd been punched. 'I plumb forgot my manners.' They was pretty rough men." She jammed her hands into the back pockets of her trousers. "That's the way I was raised. I don't know no better'n they did."

"Molly, you underestimate yourself. You're a fine woman. You treat people well. That's all good manners are, you know, treating others kindly. What are you really worrying about?"

Molly rocked back and forth on her heels. "Carson says he loves me." Her expression softened. "I took your advice and stopped fighting him. I decided I would just be me—the nicest me possible." She dropped her gaze. "He seems to like me best that way."

Lizzie laughed softly. "Of course he does. Congratulations."

Molly gave her a desperate look. "He hasn't asked me to marry him yet. Truth is, every time he starts to, I get all jittery inside and change the subject. I'm plumb scared."

"What are you scared of?"

"Fitting in. I ain't a fine lady. I don't know nothing about town life except to go to the post office or store, get what I need, and get out as fast as I can." She took to pacing again.

"Has Carson said he wanted you to live in town? Has he suggested you should change into a fine lady? Not that you aren't fine just the way you are."

Molly ground to a halt. "We have to live someplace."

"Of course."

"Not town. I couldn't stand town. I'd wither up and die."

"I'm sure if you tell him, he'll understand. He probably already does." Lizzie grinned. "Men surprise you sometimes with how much they understand."

Molly shook her head. "I'm afraid of what he'll want."

"Molly," Lizzie scolded softly. "Didn't we discuss this last time? About love meaning you trust someone? Trust Carson. He isn't going to try to make you something you're not."

Molly nodded again. "I guess I have a lot to learn about love and trust."

"And a whole life to do it in."

Suddenly Molly grinned. "Put that way it sounds fun."

A few minutes later, they heard the sound of a wagon enter

the yard. Molly left soon after, whistling as she headed toward the barn.

◆

Several days later, the doctor told Lizzie she could get up. "Be careful for a few days," he cautioned as he left.

Glad to be free of her confinement, she headed outside. The July sky was clear and bright, the sun warm enough to make her keep to the shade.

Molly strode into the yard and, seeing Lizzie against the house, angled toward her. A wide grin lighted her face.

"You look very happy," Lizzie said.

"I agreed to marry Carson."

"Good for you." She hugged her friend. "When's the big day?"

"No big day. We're getting married without all the fuss. I was hoping you and Caleb could stand up with us." She twirled around. "And Carson suggested we fix up that little house down the road a mile—you know the Rheaume place. It's been empty since the boys all went to war and the parents went back east. Carson says that way I'll have room to raise and train my horses and he'll be close for work."

"What did I tell you?"

"I prayed real hard before I would let him ask me to marry him. I knew I had to get to the place where I could trust someone. It had to start with me really trusting God. Mostly I've just tacked Him on to my life. Kinda stupid, aren't I?"

Lizzie shook her head. "Just growing up. Like the rest of us." She'd had to learn her lessons, too—to let God do His work in Caleb's life. To be true and kind and faithful and leave the rest to God. "God never fails." He'd brought healing to Caleb's heart through so many people and events. Her heart swelled with thankfulness.

આ

"I have something I want to show you," Caleb announced a few evenings later. "Are you up to a short walk?"

"Yes. My ankle is almost as good as new."

"Bring your flute."

"What are you up to?"

He grinned. "Come along and see."

He refused to say anything more as they walked hand in hand down the street. They passed the post office, the hardware store, and the feed store. Caleb pulled her toward the church.

She looked at him curiously. She really had no wish to look at the mound of dirt where Frankie lay buried, even though she knew Caleb came here often.

But he drew her after him to the exact spot.

"Look."

She lowered her eyes and gasped. "You did this?" The mound had been levelled and grass planted on the new soil to form a lush green carpet. A row of bright yellow marigolds bloomed across the head of the grave. Wild rosebushes had been pruned and transplanted to stand on either side of the cross. "It looks real nice."

"I wanted to finish it up before I left it."

She grew very still, wondering if he meant this was the end of the war.

"It's time to go forward."

She waited for him to continue.

"I wanted you to come with me to say good-bye one last time. Play something for Frankie."

She took her flute and played a march. Caleb stood with his head bowed. She finished and whispered, "Good-bye, Frankie. We'll never forget you."

"Good-bye, Frankie," Caleb echoed. "You were a good friend and a brave soldier, but you've gone to a better place." After a moment, he took Lizzie's hand and led her away, stopping under a birch tree where they were almost invisible from the street. "From now on we go forward. Together. With God's help." He pulled her into his arms. "We have the rest of our lives to live."

She wrapped her arms around his waist. Now seemed like the right time to share her secret. "And now more reason than ever to go forward."

"What do you mean?"

"I talked to the doctor, and he agrees with me. We're going to have a baby."

He tipped her head back so he could see her eyes. "A baby?"

Her eyes brimming with happiness, she nodded.

"You and me and baby." He crushed her to his chest. "What a wonderful life we'll have." His mouth found hers, saying more than any words invented could ever say.

A Letter To Our Readers

Dear Reader:

In order that we might better contribute to your reading enjoyment, we would appreciate your taking a few minutes to respond to the following questions. We welcome your comments and read each form and letter we receive. When completed, please return to the following:

Fiction Editor
Heartsong Presents
PO Box 719
Uhrichsville, Ohio 44683

1. Did you enjoy reading *Lizzie* by Linda Ford?
   ❑ Very much! I would like to see more books by this author!
   ❑ Moderately. I would have enjoyed it more if

   _____

   _____

   _____

2. Are you a member of **Heartsong Presents**? ❑ Yes ❑ No
   If no, where did you purchase this book? _____

   _____

3. How would you rate, on a scale from 1 (poor) to 5 (superior),
   the cover design? _____

4. On a scale from 1 (poor) to 10 (superior), please rate the
   following elements.

   ____ Heroine   ____ Plot
   ____ Hero   ____ Inspirational theme
   ____ Setting   ____ Secondary characters

5. These characters were special because?_____
_____
_____

6. How has this book inspired your life?_____
_____
_____

7. What settings would you like to see covered in future
   Heartsong Presents books? _____
_____
_____

8. What are some inspirational themes you would like to see
   treated in future books? _____
_____
_____

9. Would you be interested in reading other **Heartsong
   Presents** titles? ❏ Yes ❏ No

10. Please check your age range:
    ❏ Under 18   ❏ 18-24
    ❏ 25-34   ❏ 35-45
    ❏ 46-55   ❏ Over 55

Name_____
Occupation _____
Address _____
City_____ State_____ Zip_____

------- **Presents** -------

Great Inspirational Romance at a Great Price!

Heartsong Presents books are inspirational romances in contemporary and historical settings, designed to give you an enjoyable, spirit-lifting reading experience. You can choose wonderfully written titles from some of today's best authors like Peggy Darty, Sally Laity, Tracie Peterson, Colleen L. Reece, Debra White Smith, and many others.

When ordering quantities less than twelve, above titles are $3.25 each.
Not all titles may be available at time of order.